Other Mystery Novels
by Gene Breaznell

The Star of Sutherland

DEADLY DIVOTS

DEADLY DIVOTS

A GOLF MURDER MYSTERY

Gene Breaznell

BRIDGE WORKS PUBLISHING COMPANY

Bridgehampton, New York

Published by Bridge Works Publishing Company, Bridgehampton, New York,
a member of the Rowman & Littlefield Publishing Group.

Distributed in the United States by National Book Network, Lanham,
Maryland. For descriptions of this and other Bridge Works books, visit the
National Book Network website at www.nbnbooks.com.

FIRST EDITION

The characters and events in this book are fictitious. Any similarity to actual
persons, living or dead, is coincidental and not intended by the author.

Library of Congress Cataloging-in-Publication Data

Breaznell, Gene.
    Deadly divots : a golf murder mystery / Gene Breaznell.—1st ed.
        p. cm.
    ISBN 1-882593-74-X (cloth : alk. paper)
    1. Title.

PS3552.R3577D43 2003
813'.54—dc21
                                                            2003001129

            10   9   8   7   6   5   4   3   2   1

∞™The paper used in this publication meets the minimum requirements of
American National Standard for Information Sciences—Permanence of
Paper for Printed Library Materials, ANSI/NISO Z39.48-1992.

Manufactured in the United States of America.

For Susie and Betsy

A special thanks to my editor, Barbara Phillips, for the insightful way she helped shape this book. If only she could help my golf game.

DEADLY DIVOTS

CHAPTER ONE

Golf is good, golf is great, golf is a guy's wet dream. Who would commit murder on a golf course? Especially a course as inviting as Broken Oak. Where I wish I were teeing up this morning instead of investigating a murder.

As I aimed my unmarked Dodge toward the clubhouse, between a pair of plush fairways and perfect greens, I was hoping they wouldn't mistake me for one of the help and put me to work in the kitchen. Or accuse me of trespassing and usher me out. I've played at clubs like this in my dreams. There's never a blade of grass out of place, the clubhouse rivals Buckingham Palace, and the scenery beats shooting par. I can barely afford the public courses on my cop's pay. The fairways are a misnomer, the greens aren't, and the wait's longer than eternity at Pinelawn Cemetery. Which reminds me. There's a stiff somewhere out here.

Stands of tall oaks defined the fairways. Ergo the name Broken Oak, only I didn't see one looking less than imposing. Oaks that have also caused more than a few broken golf clubs, I presume. It doesn't take a club member wearing a Panama hat to figure that out. Or Sherlock Holmes in a deerstalker. You don't need to be a genius to be a good detective. All you need is a little logic and lots of endurance. That's how I lasted twenty years in homicide on Long Island, with a record number of murder convictions for Nassau County. The highest score down at the Mineola Courthouse. Opposite of golf, as the game should be played, though I also run up the score on the links too often. But murder most foul is seldom allowed on gorgeous Gold Coast golf courses like this. On priceless real estate merely a chip shot from the Sound.

The Gothic-inspired clubhouse/mansion loomed on a rise wreathed in morning mist, oozing old wealth and consummate power. It once belonged to Dame Winifred Randall, a British expatriate who made a fortune writing murder mysteries. My wife read everything she wrote. Carol read everything, anyway, God rest her soul.

I must admit to reading very few mysteries. They're like another day at the office. Or unlike it. Especially "cozies," as Carol described Dame Winifred's books. Try cozying up to the likes of John Wayne Gacey and Jack the Ripper. And all those suspects, lurking in mansions like Broken Oak's clubhouse. Or out on the moors. They can't hide from me. I can smell them, like the fertilizer on these fairways.

I tried to like Dame Winifred's work, mostly because of Carol. But the Dame's plots were too contrived and her prissy little tec was too clever. Real detectives, I often tried to convince Carol, found murder far less puzzling. Especially during Dame Winifred's era, when suspects were routinely hauled into a backroom at headquarters and convinced they should confess. When the good old "wham-bam" to the back of the head was acceptable, and admired, like a solid tee shot. Before the occasional broken bone and a couple of bruises were an issue, and we had to Mirandize everything that moved.

I parked at the front entrance to the clubhouse between two marked patrol cars, where even the club members are not allowed to park their Benzes and BMWs. I guess that's a cop perk, although I'd rather have a Beemer than a preferred parking spot.

As I climbed out of my car, a grinning uniformed cop glided toward me on a golf cart. "Stiff's out on the tenth hole, Karl," he told me, as calmly as a starter with my tee-off time.

"Where's that?" I asked.

"Hop on," he said.

"I'll walk," I insisted. "You should too."

"I know," he smiled sheepishly. "I'm getting a gut."

"I don't mean that," I said. "I mean, as a good investigator, you need to get a feel for the premises."

"Sure, Karl," he shrugged, gliding away on the cart.

I followed on foot, wondering why I had lectured him. He's a good cop with an excellent arrest record. I was feeling like Tiger Woods stalking the course. "Tiger, Tiger, burning bright," Carol would say, quoting some old poet, whenever I watched the Golf Channel, whether or not Tiger was on. She knew all the old poets but not Nicklaus, Palmer, Sarizen, Snead, Hogan, Jones. She wouldn't know Tiger if she bought a Buick from him.

Playing golf at Broken Oak, to Carol, would be a good walk spoiled. To me, it's poetry: Tintern Abbey in eighteen holes. Tees, fairways, and pins clad in one green hue, waters rolling from their mountain springs with a soft inland murmur, sportive wood run wild, connecting the landscape with the quiet sky. Wordsworth would have loved this course. I love it too, though they'll never let me play here.

The body was covered with a black tarp on the tenth fairway beside a water hazard that looked calmer than Walden Pond and could never have cost anyone a two-stroke penalty. An ambulance and two more patrol cars were parked on a nearby cart path. Several EMTs and uniformed cops milled about, all afraid to act without a superior present, watching their backs closer than the criminals.

I approached slowly, like Tiger considering a difficult lie. I've calmed down over the years. You could even call it mellowing. I used to blast my way onto crime scenes like this: siren wailing, lights flashing. Now the clues, the stiffs, the perps, and my fellow cops can wait a few extra minutes. It could have something to do with Carol dying. Made me stop and think. Whatever. We catch more killers in the crime lab these days anyway. If only the mellowing had helped my golf game. If I still didn't grip it and rip it, go long and wrong, or dub it for ten yards, believing I'm John Daly. If I could trust the club to do most of the work. If I wasn't a homicide cop who can't trust anyone.

The only civilian in sight was a silver-haired man wearing an Izod shirt, tangerine slacks, and buff-white golf shoes, like he had just stepped out of a Cadillac ad. He was surveying the water hazard and the corpse, as if trying to decide which club would best chip his ball across.

"Cordon off the hole," I ordered another uniform who was on another golf cart. It seemed that all my fellow cops could do, without a superior present, was commandeer carts. I thought of telling them, Don't get too used to these conveyances unless you're planning to hit the lottery or go on the take. I held my tongue, however, wary of the silver-haired civilian.

"Close the whole course," I added.

"Is that necessary?" the civilian asked.

"Who are you?" I asked back.

"I am Dr. Fitch," he said, like I'm the headwaiter in a crowded restaurant and being a doctor will get him a table.

"I'm Detective Kanopka," I told him, without bothering to show my ID. "I'm in charge of this investigation."

"Good for you," Fitch smirked, like "you dumb, unqualified Polack," though I'm half Irish on my mother's side. Come to think of it, I don't know too many great Irish detectives either.

"The whole course is closed," I ordered.

"Why not close just this hole?" said Fitch.

"Evidence could be anywhere." I shrugged. "You should know that."

"Of course," Fitch huffed.

"What are you doing out here, anyway?" I asked, further nettling the arrogant bastard.

"I was in the pro shop," Fitch said.

"And?"

"The greenskeeper dashed in and reported this." Fitch smirked at the stiff, as if it had cost him a two-stroke penalty.

"Of course I came at once," he continued.

"Why?"

"As I have already told you, Detective, I am a doctor."

Right. You've just scrubbed for surgery, and I might contaminate you.

"Wasn't he dead already?"

"I did not know that at the time."

"Of course."

"Now I know that he has been dead all night."

"How can you tell?"

I squatted and pulled back the tarp. Beneath it lay a middle-aged man, about my height, six feet, about my age, forty-eight. Looking somewhat like me, which is always disturbing, with thinning reddish-gray hair. But he also had a potbelly and bitch tits. I can do fifty push-ups and countless crunches.

"The obvious signs," Fitch said, as if instructing a first-year intern. "Rigor, lividity, beginning of bloat. This hazard could have a high degree of salinity."

"Lots of salt?" I asked, dumb like a fox.

Fitch raised an eyebrow. "In the common parlance, Detective."

Okay. I *am* pretty common. But I've probably seen more stiffs during my three tours in Vietnam and twenty years in homicide than most doctors. Unless they're Jack Kevorkian. I looked closely at the corpse, wincing at a deep laceration in the side of the head and at the partly crushed skull. The real difference between me and doctors is that I never got used to the stiffs.

Fitch caught my wince and said, smiling thinly, "That's a deadly divot."

Ignoring the poor attempt at golf humor, I asked, "It couldn't have happened in a fall?"

"The wound is too severe and too deep," Fitch said. "There is nothing near this water hazard that could have caused it. My guess is a nine iron or a pitching wedge."

"The blades are sharp," I said, "shaped like little hatchets, angled like this head wound. I have a great pitching wedge, a Callaway. Gets me out of the deepest traps."

"Nothing would have helped this gentleman."

"Lousy golfer?"

"And hardly a gentleman."

"You knew him?"

"His name is O'Reilly."

"You were friends?"

"Certainly not, though most of the club members know each other."

"You golfed with him?"

"Golf is a noun, Detective."

"Huh?"

"There is no such word as *golfed*."

"I'm a cop, not a college professor."

"So I see."

"So you and O'Reilly golfed?"

I can also be a wiseass.

"Never together," Fitch insisted through clenched teeth. Then he smiled thinly again, adding, "This is the earliest he has ever been out."

"What does that mean?" I frowned.

"He could never make the dawn patrol."

"I get it," I said. I sure did, having slept in my car, who knows how often, to get out early on crowded public courses before the galloping hordes.

"Can you also understand," Fitch smirked, "that it is past dawn and I should be on the second hole by now?"

"Not while I'm patrolling the course," I told him. "Patrol okay as a verb?"

Fitch smirked again. I had no idea what kind of golfer he was or what kind of doctor, but he was great at smirking.

"Very clever, Detective," he said.

I ignored the comment, noticing that the corpse was wearing a gold Rolex, ruling out robbery as a motive. It was also dressed in a blue blazer and white slacks, with the fly wide open. O'Reilly could have been relieving himself into the water hazard when somebody whacked him from behind. Or flashing the frogs. Or getting a blow job. I smiled slyly. Being a good detective also takes a dirty mind.

"O'Reilly owed me some money," Fitch said, tantalizingly, as if trying to get me back for my misuse of the language.

"You have the right to remain silent," I warned.

"Am I a suspect?" He raised an eyebrow but admitted in the next breath, "He owed me twenty."

"A small golf bet?"

"Hardly, Detective. Twenty thousand."

"Dollars?"

Fitch nodded. "That is not enough for me to kill him, if that is what you are thinking. And now I shall never get it back."

I stared at him. He stared back without blinking. He could be a good poker player. But what kind of doctor? He cared more about the course being closed than about the deceased.

"Guess you'll have to sue his estate," I said.

"There is no use," said Fitch.

My turn to raise an eyebrow.

"O'Reilly owed everyone," he explained. "He was always promoting some business deal or another, guaranteeing to get you in on the ground floor. He was flat broke, however, and I found out too late. I should have known when he was posted in the clubhouse every month, though some members pay their bills late on purpose."

"Why?" I'd be in bankruptcy court.

"So everyone is impressed by how much they spend here. The more they owe the better—an insecure, nouveau riche tactic."

"Isn't nouveau better than no riche at all?"

"To some, I suppose," Fitch sighed.

"To O'Reilly?" I asked.

"As nouveau as they come," Fitch told me.

I shook my head. Some things never make sense, even to the cleverest detectives.

"Why is he all dressed up?" I asked.

"Simple," said Fitch. "There was a cocktail party at the club last night."

"You attended?"

"My wife and I left early. And now, Detective, I would like to leave, unless you open the course."

"You speak with Mr. O'Reilly?"

"Hardly, though I could not avoid hearing him."

"Was there an argument?"

"He was loud, as usual. Also imbibing heavily."

"Drunk?"

"Possessed, as usual, with that beggarly damnation."

Even my Irish half is not fond of drunks. But I liked Fitch's superior air even less. I made him stay for more questioning and made sure the course stayed closed.

"What was he like in that state?" I asked.

"A drunk is a drunk."

"Happy? Surly? Sad?"

"Horny, to use the common parlance."

"He thought he was God's gift to women?" I know the type and I don't like them.

"He chased anything in skirts, Detective—except for his poor wife, I understand."

"Was she with him last night?"

"I did not see her. I believe they were separated."

Fitch fielded my questions like an expert. He was a cool customer. Even in the good old days of law enforcement, when tough interrogators could have hit him like a solid tee shot, he wouldn't have cracked easily.

"Ironic, is it not?" Fitch smirked yet again, like a Born Again who knows he's going to heaven and you're not.

"What do you mean?"

"Come on, Detective. He was floating facedown in this water hazard. The greenskeeper pulled him out."

"So what?"

"So a bad golfer ends his days in the same hazard where he must have lost a thousand balls?"

"That is ironic," I admitted, though I wouldn't mind dying of natural causes on a course like this. I'll never get this close to heaven. I empathized with O'Reilly lying helplessly dead on the ground, however, while an arrogant fellow club member made ghoulish golf jokes. A drunk's a drunk, but a victim's also a victim. No one deserves to die this way. And the corpse looked too much like me. My Irish half. I replaced the tarp, trying to shield the body from further verbal abuse. Dignifying the mortal remains, as my priest might put it. Since Carol's passing, I've made more confessions than I ever coerced.

"But he died on the back nine," Fitch said testily. "Can you at least open the front?"

"That reminds me of Uncle Miltie," I said.

"You mean that he and O'Reilly are both dead?" Fitch looked quizzical. A genuine smile would have cracked his face. "What does a comedian have to do with it?"

"He once asked to play only the front nine at Augusta National," I explained, "since he's only half Jewish."

"They let him?"

"Could he play here?"

Fitch's facial expression flat-lined as he said, "Broken Oak does not discriminate against anyone, Detective."

"Of course not," I said, just as flatly. Only against African Americans, Orientals, Hispanics, and a long list of undesirables including cops.

"I am only trying to play a round before my rounds at the hospital," Fitch added, apparently unaware of his wordplay.

"I'm only trying to solve a murder case," I said, aware of sounding like a snooty headwaiter squelching a snob's attempt to score a table.

Why not? It's just another cop perk, even better than parking where the country club set is not allowed. Though I'd still rather have a Beemer and be playing this course.

CHAPTER TWO

I sensed a presence looming behind and whirled as another golf cart stopped just short of hitting me.

"That's too close," I angrily told the driver.

"These things are nice and quiet," said the county medical examiner, sitting behind the wheel and grinning like an idiot.

"Too damn quiet," I said, like Gary Cooper in *High Noon*. You're dating yourself, Kanopka.

"Not too quiet for Yankee relievers," the ME said.

"I don't need relief," I told him. I haven't been blown off the mound. Not yet.

"It's a long way from the bullpen," he added.

"Cut the bullshit," I said. "Get off that thing and tell me how this guy bought the farm."

"Beautiful course," said the ME, ignoring my comment and the corpse. "I've always wanted to play here. I'd fit right in with a foursome including State Senator Molloy, Judge Harkness, and Congressman Bryce."

"They're members here?"

"It helps to be a Republican."

"And rich."

"You got that right, Detective. Guess I'll never make the cut."

Who's he kidding? He makes at least three times my salary. At least he has some hope of playing here. I'll never even make it as a guest.

"Anyway, the course is closed," I told him, as coldly as I had told Dr. Fitch. "But this murder case is wide open."

The ME finally hopped off the cart, yanked the tarp off O'Reilly like he was God's gift to cadavers, and proclaimed of the head wound, "That's quite a divot."

"So I've been told," I said.

"Made with some force." The ME looked closer.

What a genius.

"By a golf club?" I asked.

"Can't say for sure, 'til I get him back to the lab and examine him."

He always says that. I can't understand it. Even the lowliest car mechanics offer on-the-spot opinions.

"I need to know *right* now," I insisted.

"What's the hurry?"

"My men need to know what to look for."

"Why don't they look for the killer?" the ME asked, with a crooked grin.

Okay, smart guy. You think making three times my salary makes you three times as smart? I never liked the ME, but I always gave him the benefit of the doubt. He's a Yankees fan and an avid golfer. He's also young and insecure in this new position. Maybe his workload's too heavy. Maybe he dropped a bundle on yesterday's doubleheader. He needs a slap, like a crisp chip shot, to bring him back to his senses. There are other ways, however, of getting information out of smart mouths and witnesses.

"Usually, we don't know the who," I explained, as calmly as possible. "So we have to start with the what."

"I can't say for certain."

"Take a stab at it."

"I told you, Kanopka, *after* I slab him and stab him back at the lab."

Very funny. Your head's more swollen than O'Reilly's belly. You should know better than anyone else that a slab's also waiting for you someday. Hazard a guess. I won't hold you to it. You're not so important that your every word must be etched on the permanent record. Take your best shot. Like you would on any golf course.

"Could it be a nine iron or a pitching wedge?" I prodded, echoing Dr. Fitch's opinion. At least he had the guts to guess.

"Only time will tell," the ME intoned, as though he's the Delphic Oracle and I don't speak Greek.

"Could he have hit his head on a rock, or something, and fallen into the water hazard and drowned?"

"That's where he was found?"

"By the greenskeeper, floating facedown."

"We'll know, if there's water in his lungs."

"Yeah, I know. After you get him back to your lab."

"Don't be cranky, Kanopka. I'm not even on call."

"Then what the fuck are you doing here?" He's pushing me to the edge.

"I came to get a good look at the course," he grinned. "I told you, I can't afford to be a member."

"You what?"

"You must understand," the ME said. "You're also a golfer. These fairways are to die for. I didn't mean—"

"I know."

"They're spectacular, from bunker to rough, tee to green. Average golfers, you know, the lumpen of the public links, would think this place is heaven."

Lumpen of the public links? Now you're hitting too close to home, and I wish I could hit you with a wicked hook or slice one into that shit-eating grin. The way I've been playing lately, they'll never convict me. You're way out-of-bounds, but you don't even know it. I'll gladly take a two-stroke penalty to shank my next shot in your direction. Had O'Reilly's killer felt the same way? Could some slight, real or imagined, cause such violence? Why not? I'm damn close to it. I guess that murder can occur on elysian courses like Broken Oak.

CHAPTER THREE

Two scuba divers waded into the water hazard while my uniforms scoured the shoreline. "Look for a possible murder weapon," I reminded them. "Something heavy and sharp. Like a golf club."

"Also look for signs of a struggle," the head of forensics told her team. "Where this guy hit the ground. We'd like to know if he was dragged or pushed in."

"What if he did a Greg Louganis?" someone asked.

Everyone laughed, including me. Some people call me a hard-ass, but I understand the need for comic relief.

One of the divers soon brought up a golf club and handed it to the head of forensics.

"It's a five iron," she declared as the ME and I hurried over to see it.

The blade of a five iron is not as wide or heavy as a nine iron, I thought, recalling that Dr. Fitch had thought the latter caused O'Reilly's head wound. The blade angle of a five is also more closed, for hitting longer distances, plus the shaft's longer. I can hit my five about 150 yards, unless I go for more. Then I dub it for twenty. My nine's good for about seventy-five, with a higher arc due to the increased blade angle. It plops onto the green and stays there, unless I go for more. Same old story. You'd think I would have learned by now.

"No one tosses a five iron into the drink," said the ME.

"Why not?" I asked.

"It's the easiest club in the bag," he grinned.

"Not for me," I said, with a frown. Though comic relief is common, often expected at gruesome crime scenes, I'm fond of my five iron. But the ghoulish golf humor was starting to get to me. I was excited about the find until the diver retrieved six more clubs in rapid succession—some in perfect condition, others bent and rusted. One was just a shaft: what I'd be getting if I didn't come up with some tangible evidence pretty soon.

"Where's the head?" I asked, expecting the ME to tell me it was back at the clubhouse. Meaning, of course, the men's room.

"It must have snapped off," he said. "Happened to one of my clubs once, with a perfectly normal swing. Not that my swing is perfectly normal. I've got this little hitch—"

"We've got to find it," I interrupted his golf lesson. "It could be the part that killed O'Reilly."

"It could be anywhere," said the ME, suddenly more interested in all the golf balls the diver was piling on the shore.

"Must be hundreds of 'em," I said.

The ME said, "We should open a driving range."

"And a pro shop," said a young cop, swinging the five iron we found after it had been placed in a plastic evidence bag.

"Put that down!" I shouted at him. "This is not the LAPD!"

"You can still smear the prints," the head of forensics confirmed.

"And blow this whole case," I said. "Any defense attorney would have a field day with you. He wouldn't have to be Johnny Cochran."

"Sorry," said the young cop, carefully replacing the club with other collected evidence. "It's a Ping. I always wanted a set. They'd take ten strokes off my game, but they cost an arm and a leg."

"Get a Ping-Pong paddle," someone needled.

Everyone laughed, except me. The young cop had a sick wife and three kids, and he desperately needed side jobs. Owning expensive golf clubs, like the ones members of Broken Oak routinely tossed away, was a big deal. No excuse for tampering with evidence, however.

I found a distinctive heel print along the shore—obviously from a golf shoe, with one spike missing. Forensics marked it for a cast. I also found a pair of lacy panties in a nearby sand trap, the kind you see in Victoria's Secret catalogs—small, suggestive, and transparent. Carol, God bless her, used to get them in the mail and promptly turn them over to me. The catalogs, not the panties. I've been called a lot of names, but never a cross-dresser. The panties were half-buried in the sand and were almost the same color. I would not have noticed them unless the light had been just right.

As the trap was cordoned off, I took another look at O'Reilly's head wound, then at the five iron in the evidence bag. The size of the blade and the wound seemed to match. It could have administered the coup de grace, or deadly divot. But what do I know?

I headed back along the tenth fairway toward the clubhouse.

CHAPTER FOUR

The mansion, or clubhouse, was a mountain of Gothic arches and gargoyles—a dark, stone mountain, like old brownstones in the bowels of Brooklyn, where I grew up poor as a church mouse. I scampered up a sweeping stone staircase between staggered pairs of huge cast-concrete planters that looked like funeral urns. They had flowers in them, but they were also big enough for planting bodies.

I landed on a massive flagstone patio overlooking the golf course. Looking up, awed by all the finials and flying buttresses, I thought about old Dame Winifred rattling around inside. I could never live in a mansion this size, even if I hit the Lotto or Enron before the fall. All the repair costs and maintenance, not to mention astronomical heating bills, would croak this hopelessly proletarian homicide cop. These days if stress doesn't get you, it's sudden wealth syndrome.

Massive oak doors, with ornate carvings of acorns, leaves, and stags, were tucked under low stone archways leading from the patio into the mansion. Which door to choose? The lady or the tiger? Would one door admit me to a Pleasure Palace?

Would another release a club-swinging yuppie intent on making a divot in my cranium? Xanadu or Xanadon't? I only know that Carol, an English major, would not approve of mocking Coleridge.

A small sign on one of the doors read Halfway House. I chuckled to myself. In my world, halfway houses are rehab centers for druggies, foreign to most of the beau monde recovering from the rigors of the front nine with a spritzer and a club sandwich. Climbing on and off those carts and whacking little white balls out of the gentle rough must take its toll. I would not be caught dead in a halfway house, even if there was one at my public course.

The Halfway House was locked. I tried another door with a sign reading Pro Shop. It opened easily for such a heavy door. Inside was a tall, athletic-looking man, apparently alone. He was leaning on a glass display counter, reading the sports section of the local newspaper. He looked about thirty-five.

"Dang Mets dropped another one," he said with a Texas twang.

Flashing my ID, I told him, "I'm more interested in who dropped the guy out by the water hazard." I'm also waiting for the Dodgers to come back to Brooklyn.

"'Course," he drawled.

"Can you tell me about him?" I asked.

"Mr. O'Reilly?"

"Any other stiffs out there?"

"No one deserves dyin' like that."

"My sentiments exactly. But who are you?"

"Al Jones," the tall man grinned, extending a hand. "I'm the golf pro here."

"What about O'Reilly?"

"We didn't speak much," Jones shrugged. "Some folks respect my bein' their pro. Some treat me like the help."

At least you get some respect. Unlike us cops.

"Never bought much in my shop, neither."

"Lousy customer?"

"Worse 'n his handicap."

"Which was?"

"'Bout a thirty-two."

"That's not good, unless it's your waistline." Your handicap is based on how many strokes you shoot above par, which varies from course to course but averages seventy-two. I can play to a ten handicap, when I'm not trying to hit them as far as John Daly. Which means I'd have to give O'Reilly twenty-two strokes.

"That's how he liked it," Jones grinned again.

"What do you mean?"

"He only turned in his highest scores."

"Inflating his handicap like a tech stock?"

"He could play to a twenty-eight, for money."

"I know some guys like that." I could whack them with a five iron.

"He also shaved strokes, ignored penalties, was extra fond of the foot mashie."

"He kicked the ball to a better lie?" Out of the rough or a divot, off the dirt, so it sets up higher and is easier to hit.

"Only when no one was lookin'."

"How do you know?"

"Know what, Detective? The difference between golf and soccer?"

"You said he only kicked the ball when no one was looking."

"Word travels fast in these parts, pardner."

"I'm a cop," I reminded him. "Not your partner."

There's a delicate balance between loosening people up and letting them get too familiar with you.

"'Course," he said, only slightly more seriously.

"What else?"

"Mr. O'Reilly cheated at everything," Jones continued. "If you get my meaning."

"You mean, on his wife?"

"Yup."

"How do you know?"

"If I didn't, I'd be the only one in these parts."

"A real Casanova?"

"More like an old dog chasin' cars."

"Mostly reflex?"

"He wouldn't know what to do if he caught one."

"Really?"

"'Course, I'm only guessin'. He was overweight, outa shape, and he drank too dang much."

"You think he couldn't get it up?"

"He was also at least fifty."

"Hey! That's not so old these days."

"No offense, Detective. You look like you're in shape, for someone your age. Whatever it is?"

"You'd better believe it," I said, though I had not had sex, even with myself, since Carol had died a year earlier of brain cancer. I was more concerned, however, with Jones knowing so much about O'Reilly's sex life.

"So there was lots of gossip about O'Reilly?" I probed.

"He was embarrassin' to the members and a joke to the staff. Guys like him give Broken Oak a bad reputation."

"Like horny golf pros? No offense."

"Shucks. I ain't offended. Mosta these swank clubs won't hire a pro who ain't married, for obvious reasons. But they hired me anyway."

"You saying your reputation's impeccable?" I raised an eyebrow. Don't bullshit me, pardner. I'll check it out.

"Broken Oak won't hire a tennis pro, even if they're married," Jones said. "'Course, they're the worst. They had some courts here once. Plowed 'em under and made a drivin' range."

"No tennis at all? Isn't that unusual?"

"This club's for cattlemen, Detective, not sheepherders."

"Let me guess. An old Texas expression?"

"Texas born and bred," Jones grinned wider than the Lone Star State. "But I make good bread up here."

"Who was O'Reilly chasing lately?" I asked. Enough good-ole-boy crap.

"Can't say for sure." Jones looked genuinely blank.

"What would he have been doing on the golf course at night?"

"Takin' a leak? Lots of folks do it."

"Maybe he caught one of those skirts he chased and was caught in turn by her husband, in flagrante delicto."

"That mean he was gettin' laid?"

"An old cop expression. In case you haven't noticed, I'm an old cop, born and bred. Like my old man and his old man before him. And I don't make enough bread, but I'm gonna catch this killer."

"Couldn't have been an accident?" Jones asked.

"I'll ask the questions," I told him. "What about O'Reilly's wife?"

"Nice lady."

"You know her?"

"Took a few lessons from me."

"Any good?"

"She don't play yet."

"Why not?"

"Ain't ready. Wants to get comfortable with all the clubs so she don't make a fool of herself. That's not unusual. To some folks, a golf course is kinda like the Broadway stage. They want to make sure they know all their lines before goin' on."

"Good analogy," I said. "But I'm opening this show, directing all the performances, and bringing down the curtain."

I'm also not about to let any more good-ole-boy pronouncements throw me off the scent.

"By the way," I added, "the course is closed for the day."

"No skin off my nose," Jones shrugged. "I don't give lessons on Sunday anyway."

"Good," I said, meaning it. Though it felt good to keep Dr. Fitch off the course, I do not enjoy interfering with a fellow workingman's income, as long as he's not the killer.

"It ain't good for the members."

"They'll live."

"Maybe I won't."

"What do you mean? You said you have no lessons."

"Some of these members ride me so hard when the course gets closed, I can't tell if my butt's been punched or bored."

"Could one of those members be Dr. Fitch?"

"Yup."

"Why am I not surprised?"

"He coulda busted a club over my head this mornin'. Or wrapped a noose around my neck and strung me up from the rafters."

"He's the violent type?"

"My best customer for new clubs and repairs. He don't play a round without bustin' somethin'."

I withdrew a shiny new iron from a floor display. "These are expensive, aren't they?"

"Like 'em, Detective?"

"Who wouldn't?"

"You can have that set right there at my cost."

"Feels pretty good," I said, trying out my new grip. I had recently made a change, mostly for the worse. And I was tempted. My clubs are older than white dog crap.

"It'll cut your handicap in half."

Like O'Reilly's temple?

"Sand Wedge," I read the stamping on the bottom of the blade. Could a club like this stop me from playing like pastrami on rye?

"That'll get you under any ball," Jones said, "no matter what the lie."

"It's also a lethal weapon."

"Just another part of the golfer's arsenal."

"How would you use it?" I handed it to him.

He carefully set his grip with a well-practiced hip shake and shoulder wag, waving the club head, addressing an imaginary ball on the plush carpet.

"Not like that," I said.

"Huh?"

"Like Barry Bonds hits a baseball. How would you hit someone who's standing up, in the side of the head?"

Jones raised the club to his right shoulder, looking pleased to oblige. Shuffling his feet, as if digging into the batter's box. Waggling his hips and the sand wedge, ready for a Roger Clemens fastball. Suddenly taking a wicked swing at me. I flinched, but the flashing blade stopped barely an inch from my forehead.

"That's a little too close for comfort," I said, upset but trying not to show it.

"Don't worry," said Jones, his grin now wider than the state of Texas. "I can handle these things."

"You're right-handed," I observed, as calmly as possible. I felt like shouting, You could have killed me, you idiot!

"Never seen a lefty golf swing worth a damn," he said, lowering the weapon. "'Cept Phil Mickelson, who couldn't take a major if they gave it to him."

O'Reilly's apparently fatal head wound was on the left side of his cranium. If he had been facing the water hazard, relieving himself as his open fly indicated, and was hit from behind with a golf club, it would have been a left-handed swing.

"Who golfs lefty around here?" I asked, also wishing that I could play like Mickelson, though I'd win a major in my dreams.

"They're few and far between," Jones said, seeming not to mind "golf" as a verb. "Come to think of it," he added, "Dr. Fitch is a southpaw."

"You sure?"

"With a swing like one of them big ol' pretzels you get at the ballpark. A thousand lessons couldn't cure it."

"You've tried?"

"He took one lesson, quit in a huff, and busted another club. I've seen him heave a whole bag of new clubs into a water hazard."

"His temper's that bad?"

"No patience," Jones grinned. "That's bad for a doctor, ain't it?"

I had to smile. Though his jokes were cornier than *Hee-Haw* and his Texas twang annoyed me, he was oddly engaging. And handsome. He must be a hit with the ladies.

"Dr. Fitch tried teachin' me in that lesson," he added. "Told me I had a slice stance, which I don't. Couldn't remember when I last sliced one. But it stuck in my mind and messed me up for a month. I sliced more balls than the rib roast they serve at Sunday brunch."

"Been there, done that," I said. "Though I'm mostly a hooker, so to speak."

Slices glance in one direction when the club face is too open, hooks bend in the opposite direction when the face is too closed.

"It should be easier to keep them straight," I added. "The power of suggestion can be awfully strong, and there's too much time to think."

"Like detective work?" Jones said. "That's all about thinkin', ain't it?"

"Not always . . ." Sometimes it's reflex—conditioned, of course. Like letting go at the top of your swing. Like tying big guys like you up in knots.

"How 'bout it, Detective?" Jones handed back the sand wedge. "Buy this set and I'll throw in a free lesson. If you promise not to wrap a club around my neck or try to teach me."

"I'm not so patient either," I admitted, setting the club back in the display. "And I'll never be good enough for these."

"Never's a long time," Jones told me. "My daddy shot a seventy-six on his seventy-sixth birthday. 'Course he died a day later."

My old man died in the line of duty. Shot by a pimp. He was forty-six.

"Where in Texas are you from?" I asked.

"Big D," Jones drawled.

"Dallas?"

"It ain't Denver or De–troit."

"How long you been a golf pro?"

"I've done ten years," he said, as though it were prison time. I made a mental note to check his criminal record.

"Good life?"

"Mostly, I guess. Broken Oak's a pretty good club, but it ain't the PGA tour or the Skins game."

"Looks like a nice pro shop," I said. "Must bring in a pretty penny."

The surrounding shelves and display cases were loaded with designer clothes and the latest golf fashions for men and women, putting my golf wardrobe in its place. Frayed khaki shorts, T-shirts with beer logos, and a Yankees baseball cap that's older than Derek Jeter are par for the public links.

"Looks can be deceivin'," Jones said. "What with all them big sports stores these days, the members here ain't breakin' down my doors. How 'bout those irons at my cost?"

"No thanks." But I'll think about it.

"These members are loaded, but you'd think some of 'em don't have two nickels to rub together. Sure. My prices are higher. But I'm providin' a service, and they oughta support it."

"At least you get to play," I said. It was easy to like Jones. I hoped I didn't have to arrest him for murder.

"Not much," he complained.

"Play yesterday?"

"By myself, toward evening. Only a few practice holes."

"Anyone see you?"

"Slim, maybe."

"Who's that?"

"One of our caddies. Been here forever. Slim sees everything."

"What's his last name?"

"Could be Pickins, for all I know. You can find him out by the caddy shack."

"I thought it was all carts these days."

"Some folks still walk. Mostly for the exercise. Some think walkin' makes 'em play better."

"I like it too," I said. It's also a lot cheaper. "But why would O'Reilly walk the course at night?"

"That's easy," Jones grinned from ear to ear. "Mr. O'Reilly was workin' on his night moves."

"Wasn't that a song?"

"Bob Seeger, a good ole boy."

"From Texas?"

"Not sure, but I like the song. 'Bout a guy makin' out with a hot young thing in his '60 Chevy. Remember, Detective?"

The song, or making out?

"Of course I remember. I'm not that old."

CHAPTER FIVE

I got lost in the mansion's maze of anterooms and hallways while looking for the manager's office. I don't mind getting lost. I've stumbled across some great clues that way. I wandered into a mahogany-paneled parlor filled with dark antique furniture and oil paintings. Carol would have loved it. She was always dragging me to the antique and art shops over in Cold Spring Harbor, where the prices left me cold and wishing I was on the golf course. Though I do not mind window-shopping. She was always talking about the old masters, when she wasn't watching the *Antiques Roadshow*. I was always talking about the Masters in Augusta and the PGA. I'd rather have a good chip shot than a Chippendale. And Duncan Phyfe may as well be a cake mix. I'm more interested in antiques and oils when they're stolen. But I wish Carol was around to take me antiquing again. I'd hide my sticker shock, even watch PBS with her.

The parlor had a huge fireplace with a spit for roasting pigs. Not this pig. I will find O'Reilly's killer and bring him to justice without questioning suspects with a plunger handle.

I will not turn and burn eternally on the spit in a Broken Oak fireplace, while members like Dr. Fitch spit at me and my wife waits in vain on the lathe of heaven.

I heard a voice behind me, seeming to come from a marble bust of Homer.

"May I help you?" asked a small, balding man.

He must have come out of the woodwork like a termite. Or used a hidden door in the paneling like an old horror flick. His mouth barely opened as he spoke. Locust Valley lockjaw, it's called around here. An affliction on Long Island's Gold Coast that makes the rich ventriloquists. And seers, apparently. The guy knew instantly that I was not a club member and could never be one.

I flashed my ID, as I had with Al Jones. This time, however, I felt like a flasher.

"It must be about Mr. O'Reilly," he said, like there's a fly in his soup and I'm his waiter.

"Who are you?" I asked.

"I'm Randy Randall. I own Broken Oak and I manage the club. Perhaps you have heard of my aunt, Dame Winifred Randall?"

"Who hasn't?" Just don't ask me if I've read any of her books.

"Have you read any of her books?"

"Of course," I lied.

Though I had read several pages of something by the old Dame, urged by Carol, the prissy little tec, desolate settings, stuffy suspects, and red herrings on every page left me colder than gazpacho. I don't like fish either. Our house always smelled like herring when I was growing up. Charity catch, fish too ripe to sell, from a fishmonger friend of the family in Sheepshead Bay.

"Which do you like best?" Randall asked.

"They're all good," I lied again. I always fell asleep during the first few pages, then lost my place when the book hit the floor and had to start over. I couldn't even remember the title.

"I wish we had time to discuss each one," I continued, weaving a web more tangled than any of his aunt's tortured plots. But I need to ask you some questions."

"Of course," Randall smiled crookedly. "I know enough about detective work from my aunt's books to understand the procedure."

We'll see about that.

"You knew Mr. O'Reilly?"

"What a terrible accident."

"We're not so sure."

"You suspect foul play?"

"You knew O'Reilly?"

"I know all the members. I screen and approve them." Randall's mouth stayed shut, like a screen door during blackfly season.

"You approved him?"

"Regretfully."

"Why do you say that?"

"He was trying to acquire this property. And cover it with condos."

"A developer?"

"A complete misnomer, Detective. O'Reilly was a destroyer who would have razed this wonderful, historical monument to my aunt and her marvelous work."

I would raze the ugly pile too, but I'd keep the golf course.

"But you said you own the place."

"I am the major shareholder."

"This a country club or the New York Stock Exchange?"

"The property taxes and upkeep costs are exorbitant, Detective. I was forced to incorporate and sell shares."

"Which means you're subject to hostile takeovers?"

"Something like that. At least, where O'Reilly was concerned, hostile is the correct word."

"Explain?"

"He was dying to get his hands on this property."

"He got part of his wish," I shrugged.

"He got what he deserved." Randall smiled crookedly again.

"You deserve to be a suspect?" I asked.

"Hardly, Detective. O'Reilly was really no threat. I believe that he was broke, and I'm nearly solvent."

"Nearly?"

"I'd be doing a lot better if my aunt had also left me the rights to her books. An even one hundred to be exact. She began writing in the 1920s and continued to the day she died in this very parlor. She collapsed into that fireplace. The servants were off and no one found her for days. But you probably know all that."

"I know all her books were best-sellers," I said. That was all I knew. Thanks to Carol, who had read enough Dame Winifred mysteries to peg a Ph.D. on, while I failed to manage the first few pages.

"All still in print, Detective. Unlike my aunt, very much alive."

"Unlike O'Reilly," I added.

"You wouldn't believe the royalties and the movie rights," Randall continued, like O'Reilly was yesterday's news. "Unfortunately, she left all that to her favorite nephew, not to me. She had a strange sense of humor."

"I could have sold out," Randall added, brushing an imagined spot off the sleeve of his Brooks Brothers jacket. "I could have walked away with a tidy sum and no headaches. But that's not my way. Too many of these wonderful old estates get parceled out and plundered. There will soon be none left."

"Damn developers," I said, straightening my Sears necktie, attempting to egg him on.

"Very clever," said Randall. "I understand your method and your persistence. You may well be a match for my aunt's protagonist. I suppose he is somewhat dated, what with modern forensics and all. But he always got the killer."

"Me too."

"I can see that you have some of the same, shall I say, pride in your work."

"Job's a job. Now let's get back to this murder. O'Reilly had one hell of a head wound. And what you've just told me makes you a prime suspect."

"Don't be ridiculous, Detective. I've done my homework. O'Reilly was no threat. All bombast, persiflage, flat broke."

"He was wearing a gold Rolex."

"Everything's relative," Randall said, glancing at my plastic jogger's watch. Letting me know, in no uncertain terms, that the membership costs are also murder.

"Relatives are always suspect," I countered.

"Very clever, Detective. But I am in no way related to Mr. O'Reilly. Nor am I as profligate."

"That a euphemism for skirt chaser and boozer?"

Randall winced. Offended by an apt description of O'Reilly's activities, or a cop knowing a word like euphemism? "That means he spent extravagantly in the pro shop," he said, "even more in the restaurant and bar, though he was in over his head. He was also posted every month."

"Don't some of your members do that on purpose?" I asked.

"Not Mr. O'Reilly," he insisted.

"How do you know?"

"I ran a credit check." Randall smiled slightly, brushing the other sleeve of his natty jacket, checking his look in a gold-leaf mirror. "I normally respect a member's privacy and go to great lengths to protect it, but it's sort of a hobby."

"Sounds more like good business," I said, though I wasn't born yesterday. He was worried to death about O'Reilly buying him out and bulldozing this mausoleum.

"Even you must have a hobby, Detective."

"I'm a golfer," I admitted.

"Really?" said Randall, as if saying, Who isn't, these days?

"But your golf pro told me O'Reilly was a miser, and you just said he dropped a bundle in the pro shop."

"Not on clothing or equipment, as I recall. Every month, however, there was a hefty charge for lessons."

"Your pro also told me he wasn't much of a lesson taker."

"Correct. But his wife took a lesson nearly every day. Oddly, she never had a charge for carts, caddies, or greens fees. I don't think she's ever played a round."

"But she played around?" I smiled slyly.

"I understand the innuendo, Detective." Randall raised an eyebrow, though his jaws stayed wired. "You are quite clever. Quite like my aunt's protagonist. Let's just say it's par for the course, as the saying is."

"What do you mean?"

"Al Jones, tall, handsome, charming, single, in case you haven't noticed, handles a great many lessons like that."

"Is that why you hired him?" You a pimp or something? This a country club or a cathouse?

"Hardly," Randall frowned. "He is extremely discreet, and a wonderful teacher. I have never heard so much as a whisper about any indiscretions."

"Was he putting the wood to Mrs. O'Reilly?"

"Does that have something to do with a driver?"

"Was he fucking her?"

"How direct." Randall sniffed. "But I have told you all I know."

"About the virtue of handsome itinerant golf pros and bored horny housewives?"

"*Honi soit qui mal y pense*, Detective."

Say that in English, you smug pseudo-intellectual.

"Were you at the cocktail party last night?" I asked.

"Working, as usual. You would not believe my hours."

"Was Al Jones there?"

Randall shook his head.

"Mrs. O'Reilly?"

"I believe she's been away. Possibly in Florida. They were getting a divorce, you know."

I nodded. We had already informed her of her husband's untimely demise and she was on her way back from the Sunshine State.

"You sure your pro had nothing to do with their marital problems?" I probed, like a dedicated proctologist. Though Randall frowned again, I got the feeling he might enjoy a proctological exam from someone like Fabio.

"Of course," he insisted, as if sexual impropriety bothered him more than murder.

"Final answer?"

"Al Jones is the consummate professional." Randall's eyes narrowed.

"Consummate?"

"A poor choice of words, perhaps, though even gendarmerie such as yourself must understand my meaning."

"I understand that Al Jones could have slipped out to the water hazard, unnoticed in the dark, and whacked O'Reilly."

"Or I could have slipped away from the cocktail party," Randall smiled crookedly, "and done the dastardly deed."

"*Précisement*," I said, surprising Randall and myself, recalling an expression used by Dame Winifred's prissy little tec in the few pages I had read.

CHAPTER SIX

It was easy to find the caddy shack beyond the garbage compactor out behind the clubhouse. It was not easy to tell which smelled worse. Several caddies milled about or sat on overturned milk crates. All wore drab, mismatched clothing. It looked like a hobo camp. Some scowled at my approach, as if they knew I had closed the course and cut off their primary source of unreported income.

I empathized with them. Having caddied in my youth, I know how difficult it is carrying two heavy golf bags, how frustrating to keep looking for balls mishit by duffers like O'Reilly. How you get shortchanged and stiffed for tips. How looping for the likes of the terrible-tempered Dr. Fitch can be hazardous duty.

Beside the shack, a tall, skinny caddy slumped in a tattered armchair that must have come from the compactor. It was obviously his throne, and he was King of the Caddies. Emperor of the North Pole. He smoked an unfiltered cigarette and swigged something cheap from a bottle in a brown paper bag.

"You Slim?" I asked, flashing my ID like a French postcard. The other caddies shied away, as if I was checking green cards.

"Good guess." Slim grinned, displaying his rotten teeth and tossing his cigarette butt into a knocked-down campfire near his oversize feet.

"Ever caddy for Mr. O'Reilly?" I asked, wondering why Slim and his ilk were even allowed at such a posh country club. Still, I felt more at ease among these dregs than I had with Dr. Fitch and Randy Randall.

"Mr. O'Reilly, him dead," Slim said, sounding like *The Heart of Darkness*, another book my wife had urged on me, hoping to improve my police-blotter mind and get me off golf books. Or at least appreciate the work of a fellow Polack. But Joe Conrad only put me to sleep. Just like Dame Winifred.

I poked my head inside the shack and wished I hadn't. Now I understand the word *mephitic*. In addition to the stench and possibly its cause, there was a broken-down couch covered with soiled towels, some rolled up like a pillow. Someone had been sleeping there. Or taking serious naps.

"Tell me about Mr. O'Reilly," I said.

"What's to tell?" said Slim. "Dead's dead, ain't it?"

"How'd you find out?"

"The greenskeeper told me. He also said you closed the friggin' course."

"Sorry about that." I know what it's like living hand-to-mouth. "What else do you know about Mr. O'Reilly?"

Slim lit another cigarette, took another swig from the bottle in the brown paper bag, and said, "Worst hacker I ever saw. Hook, slice, hook, slice"—he nodded like a bobble-head doll—"all around Robin Hood's barn. I was always lookin' for his ball in the friggin' woods or watchin' it land in the water. Carryin' eighteen for O'Reilly was like thirty-six for anyone else."

"That bad?"

"Wherever his partner hit it, O'Reilly'd hit the opposite direction. Almost like he meant it. We zigzagged every friggin' hole, like we was rollin' papers."

"You roll your own?"

"Only with Mary Jane in 'em. Just kiddin', Detective."

I don't mind anymore. Not since it's okay for U.S. presidents, though they don't inhale, and Carol used it to alleviate the pain of her cancer.

"What else do you know?"

"The dude was a shitty tipper. Never took my advice, neither. I can play this friggin' game. Gave him some damn good tips and helped with his club selection. I know this friggin' course better than most. Also got control like you wouldn't believe. Like the ball's on a string. Anybody saw me tee it up could tell you I got a sweet friggin' swing. Coulda made the pro tour. All I needed was backin'."

"Sure," I said. Sure only that the bottle in the brown paper bag was doing most of his talking. I knew too many aging ex-athletes who coulda, woulda, shoulda. Including me. I only hope I don't start believing myself.

"Who played with Mr. O'Reilly?" I asked.

"Most everybody had a regular foursome, 'cept him. He hung around with anybody, weaselin' his way into games."

"Dr. Fitch?"

"Naw. Never. Fitch couldn't stand the bastard."

"What about you?"

Slim stubbed out his cigarette butt on the armchair where the wood frame was exposed.

"Ferocious Fitch, I call him," he said. "Hit me with his drive once when I was caddyin' for him. He should caddy for me. I hit 'em better than most of the pros."

"He meant to hit you?"

"Naw. He had no idea where it was goin'. But instead of apologizin', he nearly hit me with his friggin' driver when he flung it."

"You sure he wasn't aiming at you?"

"Naw. It was a wicked friggin' slice. I was standin' out of bounds, where I'm s'posed to. He wasn't pissed at me. He threw the friggin' club after the ball because it cost him two strokes."

"You must have been upset."

Slim shrugged. "Tipped me double that day. 'Fraid I'd sue them tangerine pants off him. I could also play the pants off him, or anybody else, if I wanted to."

I had to chuckle, then ask, "How do you know he didn't like Mr. O'Reilly?"

"Just a guess."

"Overhear any arguments, outbursts, fights?"

"Just the word around here. But don't hold that against Ferocious Fitch. Nobody liked O'Reilly."

"Really?"

"Loved to gamble. Nassaus, greenies, skins, you name it."

"What's wrong with Nassaus?" You bet on the front nine, the back nine, plus the whole eighteen. "The most you can lose for a dollar Nassau is three bucks."

"You can lose eighteen for dollar greenies, if you're always last on the green." Slim grinned as if he'd beaten me handily. "You can also lose your butt bettin' skins, if you can't win a hole."

"I bet these members can afford it," I told him.

"They don't bet chump change, Detective, and they don't abide cheatin'."

"O'Reilly cheated?"

"Know what a sandy is?"

"Sure. Out of the trap and into the hole in two strokes."

"Usin' your clubs, 'steada throwin' the ball."

"O'Reilly did that?"

"That's nothin'. Whenever he lost a friggin' ball out of bounds or in the rough, where he spent most of his time, he dropped an identical ball through a hole in his pants pocket."

"Nice guy."

"I'm gonna miss him."

CHAPTER SEVEN

I wandered back onto the course, where I soon noticed a stocky black man squatting in the middle of the sixth fairway. A par five dogleg angled by towering oaks I could never clear with my best drive but would have to try. The man was studying something in the grass and was startled to find me suddenly behind him. He jumped up, holding a screwdriver like a butcher knife and a wrench like a billy club.

"Take it easy," I told him. "I'm a cop."

"Then you should know better than sneakin' up on someone like that." He wore a black baseball cap with a big white X on the crown.

"You should know the course is closed." Sometimes I like to sound officious.

"So what?"

"So I could arrest you for trespass."

"I heard that before."

"Got a problem with cops?"

"You wouldn't believe how many times I been stopped and questioned coming and going from work in this lily-white neighborhood."

"Why didn't you tell me you work here?" I admired the hole again. Maybe I *could* clear those oaks.

"You cops know nothin' but grabbin' the first black bastard you see when there's been a crime," the man said, bringing me back to reality.

"There was a murder here this morning," I said.

"I know."

"I need to ask you some questions."

"I need to fix this sprinkler head."

"You with the maintenance crew?"

"I'm the greenskeeper."

"Really?" I may have sounded surprised, but I was only impressed with the perfect condition of the greens.

"I'm the head greenskeeper," he said, tugging down the brim of his cap and glaring at me, like Bob Gibson readying to throw a knockdown pitch.

"I'm the head of the murder investigation," I told him.

"You also wonderin' how a black man got this job?"

"Of course. It doesn't fit our racial profiling."

He smiled quirkily and said, "At least you're honest."

"For a cop?"

"Guess so." He chuckled, shifting his cap to a slightly more friendly angle.

"I'm also wondering who killed Mr. O'Reilly."

"So you go straight to the black man?"

"You got a name?"

"Vince Henry."

"Actually, you're the third person I've questioned. And the first African American. They tell me you found the body."

"Guilty as charged."

"What time was that?"

"About 4:30."

"What were you doing here so early?"

"I already told you."

"Keeping the greens? I get it. I'm only half Polack." Maybe a little self-effacing humor will make the questioning easier.

"I won't touch that one."

"Thanks. But what can you do out here before dawn, when there's no light?"

"Make sure these sprinklers are shutting off and a head hasn't popped. I got a flashlight, but I know this system in the dark. I helped design and install it. When a section of the course goes dry or gets flooded, I catch holy hell from the head of the greens committee."

"That's bad."

"So's his temper."

"Let me guess. Would it be Dr. Fitch?"

Vince Henry nodded. I noticed the power in his neck and upper torso. I also noticed a big gold ring on a thick black finger.

"School ring?" I asked.

"College of hard knocks, Detective. I had a football scholarship and was headed for the pros, 'til I blew out both knees."

"You jumped up pretty quick."

"Fear can do that."

Rage, too, I thought.

"Doesn't O.J. have bad knees?"

"He was acquitted."

"I heard he plays a lot of golf."

"Maybe he killed O'Reilly."

"You know him?"

"O.J.?"

"O'Reilly." I didn't like the look on Vince Henry's face. I hastily added, "Take it easy. I only have a few routine questions."

"Then get it over with. I need to fix this sprinkler head."

"How'd you go from football to this business?"

"I learned a lot about grass on the gridiron. Mostly with my face in it."

"How'd you find O'Reilly's body in the dark? You trip over it?"

"Come on, Detective. He was floating facedown in the water hazard. You must know that."

"Just checking."

"I got good grades in college. Some of us niggers can study as well as run the hundred."

"This may come as a surprise, but most of us cops confirm everyone's eyewitness account. How far out was the body?"

"'Bout ten yards. I had to wade in."

"We must have your footprints, along with a few others." We have so many, it'll take weeks to sort them out.

"But how could you see him?" I asked. "There was no moon. It must have been pitch black."

"I told you I got a flashlight."

"Where is it?"

"Back at the shed." He pointed at the glorious green distance. "My pants got wet. I had to change 'em."

I nodded and asked again, "Did you know Mr. O'Reilly?"

"I know most of the golfers, mostly by sight. 'Specially the ones who tear up the course."

"You mean tear it up with good scores?"

"I mean they drive their carts onto the greens, which can ruin them, never rake the traps after they dig up the sand or replace their divots. They have no common courtesy and no regard for the rules. O'Reilly was one of the worst. I called him on it once."

I'd treat this course with kid gloves if I ever got to play it, though I can't say I always do the same on some crummy public courses. At least I'm not as bad as some players I've seen, who dig up more grass than a mole and never replace it.

"How did Mr. O'Reilly react?"

"See my hat?"

"Sure."

"He told me the X must be how I sign my name, my IQ in Roman numerals, or the number in my family on welfare."

"Nice guy."

"I'll miss him."

I hate it when this happens. No one liked the victim. Everyone had a motive to kill him *and* the opportunity. There are too many questions and too few answers, like one of Dame Winifred's mysteries.

CHAPTER EIGHT

The sun was finally setting. About time. It had been a long day and I was welcoming the night, weary of questioning the country club set and a staff more concerned with the club being closed than a man being murdered. Worried about forensics giving up. Annoyed at most of my men standing around with their thumbs up their butts. So I sent them home.

I was standing alone by the water hazard where O'Reilly was found, watching shadows from the stands of tall oak gradually shroud the fairways. Considering that twilight's the best time to play golf, when the sun can't take its toll on my thin Irish skin, from my mother's side. The course is dead empty and you can play any hole you please, with no one watching your duck hooks and slices. You can also play a hole that causes you trouble over and over, until you get it down pat, until the next time you play it and have to learn it all over again. It's seldom a hole with obvious difficulty, like water hazards and extreme rough, where you know what you have to do or die trying. It's usually the subtle ones, with side-hill lies and slick greens, where you pray for divine guidance and bogies.

A patrol car coasted toward me along a cart path, stopped, and a uniformed cop climbed out.

"The scene of the crime?" he asked.

"You got it," I said.

"I've seen a lot worse," said the uniform, admiring the grounds, enjoying his play on words. These college-educated cops are clever.

"You keeping an eye on it tonight?" I asked.

"I'm your man, Detective."

"Keep it tidy so forensics can take another good look in the morning."

"Okay to smoke?"

"Just don't drop the butt, or I'll have yours. And don't go near the water. If you leave any footprints or DNA samples, you'll be my prime suspect."

"Okay to pee?"

"Do it in those bushes over there."

"You're worse than Internal Affairs," said the uniform, lighting a cigarette.

I said, "They didn't teach you not to smoke in college?"

"I got reamed for smoking at another murder scene," he said, grinning impudently.

"Fuck up forensics?"

"Worse. The victim's family complained. They said I was killing them with secondhand smoke."

"You were in their house?"

"So what?"

"I wouldn't let you smoke in mine." Especially when Carol was still alive. After a while, she couldn't even stand the smell of her medicinal marijuana.

"Would you yank me off the beat for six weeks of sensitivity training?"

"So you're the one." Oh, now I remember.

"That's me, and why I got this graveyard shift."

"Well, it's okay with me if you smoke. They're your lungs. Just don't step on anything that could be an endangered species."

"I know," the uniform smiled. "The only thing worse than messing up DNA is messing with the EPA."

"You college kids are so clever."

"You'll open the course tomorrow?"

"You planning to play it?"

"I'd give my right arm."

"What about your left?"

"You know better than that, Detective. Golf's a lefty game. That's the hand that gets the little glove and controls the whole swing. Your right only goes along for the ride. If you play right-handed, of course."

"If you're not a hooker," I added, "with a right that tends to take over."

We laughed and spoke longingly about playing the course instead of pounding a beat on it.

"All it takes is fifty grand for the initiation fee," said the uniform.

"Plus the right pedigree," I said, wondering about O'Reilly, who had comported himself, from all accounts, in a manner unbefitting even shanty Irish.

We segued from class envy and golf dreams into murder, which seemed perfectly natural, considering the way O'Reilly got whacked and the way I'd been murdering the ball lately.

"Forensics come up with anything?" the uniform asked.

"A million balls," I said. "This water hazard was loaded with them."

"These members can afford to lose 'em," said the uniform, wistfully.

"We have as many lost balls as murder suspects," I added, turning to leave.

"One more question?" The uniform held up an index finger, as if asking for a mulligan.

"Shoot."

"If a ball lands in the outline of the victim's body," he grinned impudently again, "does the player get a free drop?"

CHAPTER NINE

The quiet, mostly middle-class town called Bayville lies adjacent to the Sound on Long Island's North Shore. Bayville is not very far from Broken Oak, distance-wise. Money-wise, it's a million miles away. I owned a modest house near a small Laundromat and a big seafood restaurant called Steve's Pier, within spitting distance of the Sound. Even closer to the little graveyard where my wife is buried. I try to visit her every day.

Passing the public beach along Bayville Avenue, the town's modest main drag, I admired the lights along the Connecticut coastline across the Sound twinkling like stars. They seemed close enough to touch. On a clear day, you can see the spire of the Second Congregational Church in Greenwich, merely twenty minutes away by fast boat unless there's a chop. About an hour by car, unless the LIE's a parking lot and the Throgs Neck Bridge is in the throes of a coronary thrombosis.

I have not been to Connecticut since my wife died. We often went there together, especially in the fall, when it's too cold to hit the links, to admire the foliage and look for antique shops. I can't bring myself to go antiquing again. I can still bring myself to the links, however. In fact, I can't do without them.

When I got to my house, my tenants' car was not in the driveway. They must be stuffing their faces at the souvlaki place on Bayville Avenue or sipping suds at a local bar called Sand City. They're a young couple and they like to go out. I like them living with me, upstairs in the rental apartment I built after Carol died. When I sealed off the second story, including our bedroom, and moved downstairs to the guest room. I even added an outside stairway for them. I also stored all of Carol's belongings in the basement. I should have given everything to the Salvation Army, but I could not bear to part with anything. I seldom go into the basement anymore.

I always thought that I would die first, and not from disease or natural causes. Some wacko with a mail order assault weapon would go postal on me. Or the mob would vaporize me with a car bomb. I had nightmares about my fellow cops presenting my scant remains to my wife in a small container. When I told her about them she laughed, and said, "Kanopka in a canopic jar."

I parked, went into the house, and began making dinner. Canned tuna, raw carrots, and coleslaw from the deli. When I want something hot, I microwave a baking potato, though my Irish mom would not approve.

As I stirred some mayonnaise into my tuna, I thought about O'Reilly lying dead on that supersensational tenth hole at Broken Oak. Murder and mayo bother me. Like murder and mayhem? Like the good Dr. Fitch, ferocious Fitch as Slim the scrofulous caddy dubbed him. Fitch had a motive, though he claims not to care about the twenty grand O'Reilly owed him. He also had an opportunity during the cocktail party.

I munched a carrot, considering that the killer must have good night vision. There was no moon the previous night and, unless the ME proves otherwise, the killer needed only one stroke. An ace to golfers. A cranial hole in one to the coroner, crushing O'Reilly's skull, exposing his gray matter. Do I really want this tuna anymore?

Aces also remind me of Al Jones, who must have a good swing, who's also younger than Dr. Fitch and must have better night vision. But what's his motive, other than O'Reilly cheating at golf and being a cheapskate?

I opened a beer to go with my meal and studied my notes at the kitchen table. I usually watch *Jeopardy*, as I did with Carol most evenings. She knew the answers while I mostly showed my lack of higher education. She admitted to having the advantage of a Ph.D. I admitted that she was just plain smarter. She never teased me, though she once said if I ever made captain I'd be one big fricative. At first I thought she meant I'd be a prick. I thought a fricative was some sort of perversion. The way she laughed at me, I told her I'd coldcock any man who called me that. I was pissed until she explained it was a speech sound that Captain Karl Kanopka fit perfectly. What did I know? If she'd called me an alliterative fricative, I'd have thought it was a pervert who couldn't read. I brought her flowers the next day. She was so smart and so beautiful. I never understood why she married me. Now my eyes teared as I read my murder notes. Or was it the onions I chopped for my tuna?

I opened another beer to go with my notes on Randy Randall, Vince Henry, and Slim. Randall could have murdered O'Reilly to keep his Aunt Winifred's historic estate from being carved up and condoed. Vince could have rung his chimes for racist remarks or driving a cart onto a green. Slim could have whacked him for being a lousy tipper. This case could need a case of beer.

One six-pack later, though Carol would have scolded me, I concluded that anyone could have murdered O'Reilly. He was obviously an outcast, Carol would have called him a pariah, who nobody liked. Whom nobody liked? Carol knew but would never correct me. All I know is that O'Reilly, like me, was all alone in life. I wish I could get inside his head, prior to the deadly divot, of course. He drank too much; I've been doing the same thing since losing Carol. Though alcohol has not ameliorated my grief, as Carol would have put it, neither has it helped me solve any murders or justify God's ways to man.

CHAPTER TEN

I heard the sound of footsteps in my sleep. Heavy footsteps on loose floorboards. *Creak, creak, creak . . .*

I tried waking up but was too thick with sleep, drugged, it seemed, from tiredness and too many beers. I tried harder, clawing my way toward consciousness, but the murkiness in my brain melded with the murkiness in my bedroom. I had fallen into a black river and could not find the surface. With a terrible headache. Was I having a stroke? Why was I waving my arms in the darkness? Was O'Reilly's killer coming after me, wielding his five iron? What an irony. I always liked that club, comfortably between my nine and two irons, consistently good for 150 yards. Why can't the killer whack me with the two? I never know where that's going.

The creaking continued, followed by moans, as if someone had been struck and lay bleeding. But it wasn't me. I keyed on the moaning and finally forced myself awake, flat on my back in bed, staring feebly at the black ceiling. Finally realizing that the creaks and moans were coming from the young couple upstairs making love. According to my alarm clock, it was midnight.

Their moans carried out their open bedroom window on the sweet summer night breeze, sifting seductively down through mine, along with their creaking bedsprings and a cadence that beat the band. Both in the throes of enviably long orgasms, beyond anything I can remember accomplishing in that same room, on the antique sleigh bed that my wife termed our "love sled," which is now somewhere in the basement.

Ah, youth. Now I only have a headache.

The moaning suddenly stopped. All was quiet. They must both be asleep, leaving me, like an unrequited lover, staring at the black ceiling, wondering how I'll get back to sleep. Another six-pack? No way.

I got up, took two aspirin, and went back to bed. I still couldn't sleep. I reached for one of my favorite golf books but held back. Once I start reading *A Good Walk Spoiled*, by John Feinstein, I can't stop. It puts me on the PGA Tour, more like a fly on the wall than a great player, of course.

I remembered Dame Winifred Randall's little mystery. The one my wife had recommended, trying to get me off golf books, though she liked Bagger Vance. That could do the trick. With its stuffy settings, predictable plots, antiquated prose, I'd soon be sawing logs and sending pleasurable snores to the young couple upstairs. I could not remember the title but recalled tucking it into a storage box in the basement.

In the basement, I miraculously found the right box. The book was wedged at the bottom. I dug it out, trying not to cry when I saw Carol's summer dresses carefully pressed and folded.

The cover and first fifty pages were missing. Who needs them anyway? The first fifty pages of a manuscript Carol had sent to agents and editors meant nothing except a few form rejections. There was mostly no response, though she included SASEs. Her response to the rejections was stoic. I would have bitched and moaned.

There was something appealing about the wretched little paperback, something about its frail, yellowed pages. Some of it had crept into my subconscious, like the moans of pleasure from upstairs. After a painfully ponderous opening, Dame Winifred's prissy little tec, on vacation, finally discovers a body out on a moor. He was always on vacation, which would not endear him to hardworking homicide cops.

What was his name? I wracked my brain. It sounded like cool, though he was totally uncool. Cool is Harrison Ford, Eddie Murphy. But his name was French, spelled almost like cool. Coul-something. Of course. Couloir, Peter H. I was pleased with myself to remember, as if I'd remembered some witness or suspect.

I brought the book upstairs to my bedroom and lay with it on my bed. A poor substitute for a highly orgasmic young wife, or even an old blow-up doll. At least it would put me to sleep. A few more loose pages fell out. When I nod off, I thought, and the book hits the floor, the binding will surely break.

I'll start in the middle, like most of my murder cases, when the body is discovered, between the killing and catching the killer. In medias res, Carol used to say. I think that's right. She was always using arcane terms and slipping them into her writing. No wonder she couldn't get published.

Though the book looked and smelled like the Dead Sea Scrolls, something other than its use as a substitute sleeping pill suddenly appealed to me. Carol had touched and turned every page, several times over. I was finally sharing the book with her, wishing I had finished it way back when, not disdained Dame Winifred's work in general and not ridiculed her prissy little sleuth. What a putz I had been.

I began reading in the middle of a sentence at the top of page 51.

. . . Couloir carefully rolled the body over, noticing a bullet wound in the back . . .

That's pretty silly. You just don't do that. In fact, you never did, even back in the 1920s, when this was written. You waited for the ME, the coroner, a doctor, or whatever they called a forensic pathologist back then.

I read on, recalling my wife trying to explain, "It's the overall story that counts. Not cop minutiae and the gospel according to Kanopka."

More pages were missing throughout the book. The plot got even choppier. But I could not help noticing a strong similarity between the murdered guy on the moor, a brash American named Marty Phelps, and O'Reilly at Broken Oak. Nobody liked either of the deceased, as page 56 explained.

. . . the Earl of Cranbrook told him that he had been hunting out on the moor that morning when he and his gamekeeper discovered the corpse. But they failed to report it until noon because, according to the Earl, "There was no point in ruining a good grouse hunt." He was aloof, arrogant and unaware, or uncaring, that he had obstructed the investigation. Such incredible callousness, thought Couloir, invokes suspicion . . .

Any detective knows that. But this earl of Whatchamacallit's not wanting to louse up a good grouse hunt over a mere murder on his property was just like Dr. Fitch being more concerned about missing his regular golf game than about O'Reilly. They fit each other to a T. Hey, good golf pun.

Beyond a few more missing pages, I learned of the earl's passion for shooting and his weapons collection.

. . . The Earl carefully withdrew the shotgun from its green velvet nest in the burled walnut display case. He passed the weapon to Couloir, wiping a slight smudge on the hand-carved stock with a sleeve of his silk waistcoat. He looked, for all the world, like a loving mother attending to her infant. "It's a Smithers 18 gauge, wonderful craftsmanship, his finest example . . . Like it, M. Couloir?" The detective nodded, though he knew little about guns . . .

I shook my head in disgust. A cop knowing nothing about guns is no cop in my book. Lucky I always fell asleep before this page in the past, or I would have tossed the little tome into the trash.

". . . I know only that a shotgun was not the murder weapon," Couloir stated. "By virtue of the neat entry wound." He handed it back to the Earl, and drifted toward the display of his pistol collection . . .

Maybe he does know something about guns, I reconsidered. Maybe he was only playing dumb so the earl would let down his guard. I've done that, though never to an earl. This book's getting better. It could really get good if Couloir has the balls to use the good old wham-bam on this suspect, which was allowable in those days. I'm not sure about knocking around the nobility, however.

". . . See any to your liking?" asked the Earl.

"That one," Couloir answered, pointing at the only vacant space.

"Ah, but that one was stolen some time ago. A Webley-Vickers, .44 caliber. Not rare in the least, but I cherished it as a souvenir from my service in the Crimea. And I know what you're thinking, Detective."

"Please tell me."

Smiling, the Earl summoned his butler into the study. He ordered some brandy before explaining, "You believe that my missing Webley-Vickers may have been the murder weapon."

"Précisement . . ."

There's that word again. Damn Frenchies complicate everything, including our wars with Iraq. After we saved their bacon, paté de foie gras if you prefer, back in the Big One. Well, maybe they're not so bad. Though they don't have any great golfers, my wife and I had a great time in Paris.

I read on, hoping Dame Winifred was not so trite as to make the butler do it.

CHAPTER ELEVEN

It was tough getting up the next morning after staying awake too late reading the little mystery. I also forgot to set my alarm. The young couple scurrying down the outside stairs woke me.

I stumbled out of bed and staggered into the bathroom. Usually I was up and off to work much earlier, even after Carol and I had stayed up late moaning and squeaking the bedsprings. Maybe that's why she married me. Now I'll never know. It seems so long ago, when we were young. Before two incomes and scurrying to work were more important than staying up late making love. Now I'm beat from merely reading late.

I parked in a handicap space at the Nassau County Medical Center in East Meadow. Half of the handicap tags are undeserved anyway, or used by friends and relatives. Some of the so-called handicapped I've seen leaping out of their cars in the blue spaces could win the Olympic high hurdles. There were also no other spaces, and I do have a handicap. In golf, anyway.

The medical center was packed with everyone dying to get in, like most of Long Island, since Levittown supplanted the potato farms. If I lived in East Meadow, I mused, I'd be dying to get out. When I buy the farm, plant me next to Carol in the little cemetery behind our house in Bayville. Then we'll spend plenty of time together, so she can't complain about playing second fiddle to homicide or being a golf widow.

I knew the way to the ME's office, having been there too many times before. An assistant greeted me, saying, "Long time no see, Detective."

"Not long enough," I told her.

She smiled and said, "He wants you in the lab."

"Of course," I said, pausing. Autopsies bother me, though back in high school I was a part-time operating room attendant. I slabbed 'em, the surgeon stabbed 'em. I saw hundreds of operations and even helped by holding limbs and repositioning the patient. Mom wanted me to be a doctor, but my old man knew better. "You're a born cop," he told me. "Just make sure the perp needs the doctor, not you."

The ME failed to notice me when I entered the lab. He was hunched over an autopsy table, literally up to his elbows in O'Reilly's chest cavity. I stood by quietly.

Holding up O'Reilly's liver like a trophy, the ME said triumphantly, "Slightly cirrhotic, eh?"

"But the booze didn't kill him," I countered, hoping my own heavy drinking of late was not turning my liver into a loofah. I also hoped the ME would not try some pun about O'Reilly being a high liver.

"It would have, eventually," he pronounced, slipping the organ into a stainless steel container.

"It was the head wound, right?"

"No doubt," the ME said. "But I have to look everywhere."

"Of course."

"You should know that," he added. "Weren't you in medicine?"

"If you call medicine mopping floors in the OR at Brooklyn General."

"I remember," he said. "Back in high school?"

Why had I told him? I never liked this guy.

"You didn't want to be a doctor?" he said.

"It was pretty glamorous," I said, recalling the blood, guts, and sutures in my mop bucket.

"Much like forensics," said the ME, diving again into the chest cavity.

"Almost finished?" I asked. More than twenty-four hours had passed since the murder. The killer's trail, if there was one, was getting colder than the stainless steel autopsy table.

"Canoe's not completely bailed," the ME grinned.

I never liked that expression, though the insides of eviscerated human chest cavities do resemble wood-ribbed canoes. It renders our essence too precarious and hollow.

"Can I get some coffee?" I asked, as the smell began to get to me.

"Stick around," the ME said, stabbing at something in the chest cavity, wanting me to stay and appreciate his work, or puke my guts out. I stayed. Not for either of his reasons. I knew that here in his laboratory, unlike on the links out at Broken Oak, he was more likely to offer an opinion. I also knew that opinions are often more important than medical facts.

"After you've autopsied a woman," the ME said, patting what was left of the chest with a bloody glove, "live tits never look better."

"Let's stick with O'Reilly," I told him, though I tend to agree with him. "What else can you tell me?"

"Look at this—" He indicated the head wound.

"I've seen it."

"No," he insisted. "Come over here."

I went to the head of the table, eyeing the corpse from all directions, as if lining up a long putt.

"Like my excavation?" the ME asked, like a kid showing off a new toy.

"You've—"

"Enhanced it?"

"I suppose you could say that."

"Sorry about the brain being gone."

"Me, too," I lied. The word *brain* makes me cringe since Carol died.

"I can show it to you later."

"That's okay."

"It's on the baloney slicer. We're cutting cross sections. That five iron really dug into it."

"You sure it was a five iron?"

"The blade angle, width, thickness, depth, they all check out. There's also a mark from the shaft." The ME pointed to a slight indentation on a shaved section of the scalp.

"This wound is on the left side," I observed, "along the temple above the left ear."

"Which means he was hit from behind, by a lefty."

"But the club was right-handed."

"And the assailant was over six feet tall."

"How do you know?" Does political correctness know no bounds? How about calling him a cold-blooded killer instead of an assailant?

"We have tests, measurements, angles, for all heights and weights of assailants with all kinds of weapons. This guy had to be six-three or six-four. We can often calculate it to the centimeter."

"That's great," I said, "but not enough for a conviction." I know of such tests. They're often uncannily accurate or hopelessly wrong.

Ignoring my comment, the ME continued, "Think of a baseball swing. Elbows up, as well as the club head, like a Louisville Slugger."

He showed me his baseball swing. Like a kid playing sandlot, with the corpse as home plate.

"What about the wrist angle?"

"Only a slight variable. You'd be surprised."

"And the width of the stance?"

"Also slight."

"How about bending the knees? Some crouch, some stand up straight. If you ask me, the killer could be any height."

The ME looked at me as if to say, Who asked you?

"Okay," he admitted. "Maybe we only get it to the inch and not the centimeter."

"Is that still good?" I said. "I don't understand the metric system."

"You and most of this country," said the ME, off the sand-lot and back on his lectern. "At least you can understand the assailant had to be strong. It takes a lot of force to penetrate the skull so deeply. We use state-of-the-art equipment to measure it exactly."

"A burly lab technician whacking casaba melons?"

"They do say you're a wiseass, Kanopka."

We both had to laugh.

"Could the killer be a woman?" I asked.

"I've already considered that," the ME countered, annoyed at the thought of a flatfoot being one step ahead of science. "I'm sure we both know some very strong women who could whack you for looking sideways at them."

"Or for peeing into a water hazard? Like our victim?"

"We don't know that."

"But his fly was open." Don't lab techs open their flies to pee? What's he wearing under that lab coat?

"So what?"

"Was his bladder empty?"

"Of course. That's life, when you're dead."

"You mean he could have let go after getting whacked?" After all this time with homicide, I'd forgotten that little fact.

"Involuntary reflex."

"So when did he die?"

"Midnight, or pretty close."

"Anything else about the murder weapon?"

"Funny you should ask." A sudden gleam in the ME's eye told me he had discovered something important. Something the average flatfoot could never figure out. "We found traces of ash in the wound."

"Ash?"

"From burned wood. Plus some chlorophyll."

"From mouthwash, I suppose?"

"From grass."

"The kind you smoke?"

"You got me, Kanopka. I tried it a time or two in med school, but you'll never convict me. I never inhaled."

"Now who's the wiseass?"

"Okay. It was grass like you find on the golf course, along with some dirt."

"A club someone played with?"

"What else would you do with it?"

"Kill." I shrugged, ruling out the shiny new irons from Al Jones's display rack. "Do any of the clubs we found in the water hazard or out on the course match?"

The ME shook his head.

"How about the footprints?"

"We're still working on them. There are too many indistincts and partials."

"Dead end?"

"Maybe not."

"What else have you got?"

"One good heel print from along the shore."

"And?"

"One spike's missing."

"That could be huge."

"Let's hope so. Good footprints often lead to convictions."

"But there's one problem," I considered aloud. "If O'Reilly was murdered long after the course was closed for the evening, why was the killer wearing golf shoes?"

"He played until dark and was looking for a lost ball?"

"'Til midnight?"

"Golf can be obsessive," the ME said.

"Don't I know," I said, wondering if I had time to hit a bucket or two at Eisenhower Park driving range.

Maybe I was going nowhere, despite modern forensics. Which bothered me more than this finicky ME, who couldn't bust a pricey piece of lab equipment. When his lab work's done, so is he. But my job's just beginning. No matter what they say these days, despite DNA and CSI, the legwork of your average gumshoe far outdistances lab work. After all the evidence is in, someone still needs to catch these creeps. With fast feet and "sizzle in the synapses," a term Dame Winifred Randall's prissy little tec is overly fond of using. With both hands tied behind our backs, where the good old wham-bam is concerned, now that the criminal's rights are more important than the victim's.

"Anything on the condom and the panties we found in the sand trap?" I asked.

"Semen and pubic hair. In that order. We're working up the DNA."

"Maybe it's O'Reilly's?"

"You think the killer caught O'Reilly with his wife, or girlfriend, in flagrante delicto?"

"Possibly."

"Or practicing their sand shots together?"

"With her panties down."

"I can tell you it wasn't our corpse's condom, with no testing whatsoever."

"How?"

"It's a magnum."

"So what? So's my pistol."

"Not this guy's. Perhaps you're not familiar with a magnum condom."

"Of course I am. They're extra-large. I tried one once but split it."

"Me too," the ME chuckled. "We're both big hitters. Long off the tee, and otherwise. But our corpse was carrying a putter in his pants."

"Really?"

"Take a look."

I took a sidelong glance at O'Reilly's pubic region, like you do in men's locker rooms. His penis was so small it seemed Lorena Bobbitt had attacked *him*.

CHAPTER TWELVE

O'Reilly had a sprawling house on Dosoris Lane in Lattingtown. Dosoris means widow's dowry, my wife once told me. It comes from the Latin word for gift. It seems appropriate, since O'Reilly's wife now owns the house. Usually murder lessens the spirit of giving.

Mrs. O'Reilly could be sitting pretty, unless there's a whopping mortgage and massive debt, as Randy Randall supposed. She could be flat-broke homeless. I was still waiting for the credit report. D&Bs can take longer than DNAs. Either way, however, she had a motive for the murder and could have hired the killer or put someone up to it. In absentia is no alibi. Do they mean the same thing? Carol would have known. She also taught Latin, though not to me. I was fearful that dead language, often used to flummox the unsuspecting, when combined with my detective's devious mind, might turn me into a lawyer.

I noticed that O'Reilly's driveway had recently been resurfaced, leading me to believe that he may have had some money. I had gotten an estimate for my own driveway, much shorter and narrower, and abandoned the project. It seemed the contractor, who was driving a new Lexus, paved with greenbacks instead of blacktop. He was even the friend of a fellow cop. So much for perks.

O'Reilly's driveway was lined with impatiens. But flowers are cheap, except for the planting and tending. Unless you do it yourself. Like me, though I don't tell too many people. Nor do I tell them I do it out of deference to Carol, a real horticulturist who could grow magnificent Maigold roses.

Who tended these beds? I wondered, pulling into O'Reilly's driveway, parking behind a Mercedes by the front door. Cars are no indication of wealth, however. The richest guy at Broken Oak, I learned from a uniform, as he longingly lampooned the upper crust, owns a food conglomerate and several talk radio stations, conservative of course, but drives a battered old Chevy station wagon.

I had expected to find a few cars here belonging to friends and mourners. The deceased was not well-liked, putting it mildly, so I did not expect a full-blown Irish wake.

I got out of my car, walked to the front door, and pressed the buzzer. Waiting for someone to answer, I noticed the exterior of O'Reilly's domicile was pretty spiffy. The roof looked new, the gutters seemed in good shape, no paint was peeling. Was O'Reilly in bed with the mob? I had to consider it. Even Tony Soprano plays golf and might prefer a five iron to a firearm when making a hit.

I hit the buzzer several more times. Still no answer. Concluding the house was dead, I decided to look around, hoping there were no guard dogs. I had no mace. And giving guard dogs the good old wham-bam can cost a hand.

I followed a brick-in-sand pathway leading behind the house. The property was big, with plenty of trees and shrubbery. It was also quite private. It looked like O'Reilly had it made until his untimely death. What better way to go, however, than with a fancy address, a gold Rolex, and a belly full of country club booze?

I came to a swimming pool with sparkling sides and shimmering water beyond a gate through a tall privet hedge. The pool reminded me of one in a TV commercial where a guy in a Speedo dives in and the shadow of an airplane glides silently across the water. I did not like flying before 9/11. And I don't like swimming all that much. But I like the idea of gliding through crystal-clear water better than slogging through the backwaters of crime.

Stepping silently into the gate through the hedge, wary of guard dogs, I peered around a leafy corner. Instead of seeing a guy in a Speedo, I saw a woman bouncing up and down on the diving board. She was also no dog, built like an aerobics instructor, and completely naked. Her ample breasts stayed magically suspended, like twin headlights coming at me, as the rest of her body bounced. And her high beams were definitely on.

She did not see me, however, lurking like a pervert in the privet hedge. She continued bouncing, finally performing a perfect one and a half with no splash on entry. I gave her a ten for everything: dive, tits, overall tan. I would have enjoyed watching a repeat performance but, feeling like a peeper, I stepped back from the hedge and called loudly through the portico, "Anybody home?"

I expected her to shoo me away. Or shout for me to wait while she scrambled for some clothes.

"Come in," she said calmly, as though I should strip and join her.

I stepped through the gate and found her bobbing in the pool, still naked and unaffected by my presence. I flashed my ID, like a middle-schooler showing off a condom.

"Now I feel safe," she said, with a wry smile.

I said, "I'm looking for Mrs. O'Reilly."

"That's me," she chirped, still bobbing, her breasts, like twin torpedoes, barely breaking the water's surface.

"Sorry about your husband," I said, trying to concentrate on her eyes that were bluer than the water.

"Me too."

Really? She had some way of showing it. She could also be drunk, on drugs, or trying to drown.

"I have to ask you some questions," I told her.

"Ask away, Detective."

"Wouldn't you like to—"

"Put on some clothes? Who would feel more comfortable? Me or you?"

"Well—"

"I said I'm sorry, but I'm not shattered. Does that make me a suspect?"

She glided toward the diving board, slowly breast-stroking, also exposing her shapely buttocks. I suddenly felt a stirring below my belt, my first erection since my wife died. But now was not the time to regain my sexual prowess.

"Any spouse is a suspect," I said to a deck chair, trying to ignore my inconvenient tumescence.

She laughed and did a surface dive.

"Were you and your husband separated?" I asked, as she resurfaced.

"Getting divorced," she said, spitting water. "My husband was a pig, Detective. I don't mean like a cop. I like cops."

"I understand."

"You sound more like a shrink than a cop."

Wishing that something else would shrink, I sank into a chaise longue with a raging hard-on. If Mrs. O'Reilly continued bobbing or did another surface dive that winked at me, I'd explode and split my pants.

"Who else didn't get along with your husband?" I tossed out.

"Where should I begin?" she said.

"Wherever you like," I told her. Just don't get out and bounce on that diving board again.

"But the list is so long, Detective . . . From bimbos he hustled and dumped through all his business swindles, including everyone at Broken Oak."

"Dr. Fitch?"

The mere mention of the good doctor's name caused the pressure to ease in my pants.

"I don't know him," she said, performing some underwater aerobics.

"You sure?" I said, wishing I were a carp instead of a cop.

"Or many of the other members," she added.

What about Al Jones's member? Do you use the overlapping or the Vardon grip? There must be something going on with all those lessons and never playing a round—of golf, that is.

"When we first joined Broken Oak," she continued, "I went there a lot. Until I happened to ask some old biddy, just trying to make conversation, why there was no swimming pool. You know the type. She had hair like a blue helmet and sat around all day sipping tea laced with sherry, or whatever, dishing dirt on anyone and everyone. Anyway, she told me that pools were entirely too noisy and attract kids like flies to shit. Of course she didn't say the s-word, which must be tough for an anal-retentive. She was also letting me know, in no uncertain terms, that I'm not even on the bottom rung of her social ladder. It's her attitude in general, and that whole club's, believing that new money stinks on ice and old smells like honeysuckle. And they must hate kids . . ."

She spoke so freely and fast, she could have been on speed. I had to chuckle. When Carol got riled up, she could also go on a roll, spitting venom, swearing like a trucker. But she'd never dance naked on my grave.

"So you quit going?"

"Wouldn't you, Detective?"

"What about all your golf lessons?"

"Mind turning your back? I'm getting out."

Why is she suddenly modest? I turned my back, since the only weapons she carried were those torpedo-like tits, and noticed Nelson DeMille's latest best-seller lying on a deck chair with a cell phone as a bookmark.

"You see, Detective, and please don't turn around yet, I only took lessons in the hope of being able to play with my husband. I wanted to please him but couldn't get the knack."

He must have been deaf, dumb, and blind.

"Golf is so difficult," she added. "After my run-in with helmet hair, lessons were the only reason I ever went to Broken Oak. But I never played."

"Why not?"

"I would only have embarrassed myself. You can turn around now."

"But you look athletic," I said, facing her again.

She wore a short terrycloth robe, letting it flap open occasionally.

"I'm a good swimmer and diver," she told me, "but making solid contact with that little white ball eludes me. Sometimes I miss it by a mile."

"Maybe Al Jones is a lousy teacher."

"Oh, no. It's that silk purse out of a sow's ear sort of thing."

"Are you and Al Jones lovers?" I hoped my abruptness would startle her into a confession.

"Why, Detective," the widow O'Reilly said, sealing her robe shut. "You do get right to the point, don't you?"

She pulled a pair of mirrored Ray-Bans from a pocket in the robe and put them on.

"Have I touched a nerve?" I asked.

"I wasn't fucking the golf pro," she said evenly.

"You can also get to the point."

"I was also in Florida when my husband was murdered."

"We know."

"And I just got back."

"If you don't mind, I'd like to look inside the house."

"Got a search warrant?"

"Do I need one?"

"In case you haven't noticed, Detective, I've got nothing to hide."

Believe me, I noticed.

"Mind if I call headquarters first?" I asked. "They like me to check in once in a while."

"You can use my cell phone," she said. "But don't lose my place. Ever read Nelson DeMille?"

"Only Byron Nelson."

"Who?"

"They called him Lord Byron."

"Sorry. I've never heard of detectives liking poetry."

"I'm sensitive," I said, trying not to grin like an idiot. Or admit that Byron Nelson was a great golfer, lord of the links, with a swing that's poetical.

"I'll meet you inside," she said, walking toward the house on her toes. Like a ballerina—or a pole dancer.

I reached for her cell, carefully keeping her place in the book. Instead of calling headquarters, however, I hit the redial button. After only one ring, a man answered. I recognized the Texas twang.

CHAPTER THIRTEEN

We found no criminal record for Al Jones. We're also checking his work history. It's not easy. Plenty of golf pros work off the books occasionally, like plenty of cops. Jones also bounced around a lot, like balls I've sliced off holes next to highways. I once hit one onto Old Country Road from Eisenhower Park that's still bouncing. I have my Johnny Miller moments, but I'll never win the U.S. Open.

After checking out O'Reilly's house and finding nothing unusual, I drove back to Broken Oak. It was Monday and the club was closed as usual. But I hoped to corner Randy Randall and come up with a copy of Jones's résumé.

Except for a few forensics people tidying up on the tenth hole, the golf course was dead empty. I was pleased to investigate in relative peace, without Dr. Fitch looking over my shoulder, dunning me to let him play, or Vince Henry, the greenskeeper, examining his irrigation. Courses need occasional rest to recover from duffers like O'Reilly. Could the gods of golf have whacked him for disrespect, aided and abetted by the ghost of Robert Trent Jones? I'll open it to-morrow anyway. There's as much chance of finding more evidence as one of these members finding a moment of silence for O'Reilly before teeing off.

I found Randy Randall in his office, a cramped, windowless room off the kitchen, the butler's pantry when Dame Winifred lived here. No wonder the butler always does it, with pantries like solitary confinement at Riker's Island.

Randall was seated at a rolltop desk, intently studying some papers, holding a ballpoint in his right hand. I cleared my throat to get his attention.

"I told you the club's closed," he said, before looking up.

"You didn't tell *me*," I told him.

"Oh, it's you. I thought you were a salesman."

"Selling what?"

"They're all the same. Who knows? How did you get in? I thought I locked everything."

"Not the front door," I said.

"That lock's a little tricky," Randall said. "I should have it replaced. It's fooled me before. We recently had intruders who took most of the liquor and a cash box I kept in here. Nothing was damaged, thankfully. They could have entered through the unlocked front door."

"It's still called a break-in."

"The police thought it was some local kids, or our caddies. They never found out. No offense, Detective, but your department did not try too hard."

"Do any of the members try to get in here on Monday?"

"Occasionally. I always refuse them, though some can't seem to take no for an answer."

"That must bother you."

"Hardly, Detective. Their insistence, for lack of a better word, is how they got where they are."

I can think of some better words. But I can't let this case get away from me. It's time for a verbal wham-bam.

"Cut the bullshit," I said. "Someone else was just in here and left the front door unlocked."

"No. Really—" He looked genuinely puzzled.

"Let me get this straight. You live here all alone?"

"If you can call it that. After all the late dinners and cocktail parties, when the staff's cleaned up and gone home, before the morning shift comes in and prepares breakfast for the early golfers, I do have an hour or two to myself. I must confess to liking January best, when the club's completely closed. And I usually like Mondays."

"Your aunt Winifred also lived here alone?"

"She had help."

"Was she sleeping with any of them?" Another wham-bam, trying to loosen his Locust Valley lockjaw.

"Come on, Detective. You can't besmirch a progenitor of the mystery genre."

"Huh?"

"My aunt was constantly sleeping with the help. You've obviously never heard of the 'Randall Scandals' and 'Randy Dame Winifred.' She was caught in compromising positions with servants and royalty."

"Really?"

"She was always in the tabloids."

"Tell me more about your aunt." I'm not sure why I wanted to know.

"She was very beautiful. You may have noticed her portrait in the foyer."

The life-size full portrait Randall referred to was the focal point of the huge entrance hallway he modestly termed a foyer. Randy Dame Winifred, at least in oil, if not on the printed page, had certainly caught my jaundiced eye.

"She was no dowdy dame," I said.

"That's one way of putting it. You noticed the plunging neckline?"

"Noticed?" I said. "I nearly fell in."

"*Quelle décolletage,*" said Randall, trying to sound like a tit man. Though he looked and sounded more like his aunt's prissy little tec.

"Few know what a femme fatale she was," Randall continued.

"Who was the artist?"

"Some unknown, but he did a good job. If she were only alive and writing today."

"She'd look damn good on a book jacket."

"I meant her writing, Detective. The tragic part of the Randall Scandal was her cuckolded husband blowing his brains out. That was partly why she came to this country. When she was here, she calmed down considerably."

"Maybe that's why the book I'm reading is so boring." I tried a different angle to raise his hackles, hoping for a slipup.

"Which book?" he asked.

"This may sound foolish, but I don't know the title. It belonged to my wife. She was a big fan, read everything of your aunt's. But the cover and a bunch of pages are missing."

"What's it about?"

"A guy's been shot in the back on a moor surrounding a big estate like this."

"A brash American?"

"I think his name is Phelps."

"Martin Phelps?"

"That's him. The estate's owned by a gun enthusiast called the earl of something."

"That's the earl of Cranbrook. Your book, Detective, is *Murder on the Moor.* One of my aunt's most famous works."

"Don't tell me the ending."

Randall was pleased to get me off the investigative track for the moment, maybe because *Murder on the Moor* had a lot in common with O'Reilly's murder. There could be a clue in that book that would finger Randall. The settings were uncannily similar, as were some of the characters.

"Tell me about Al Jones," I told him.

"I've told you all I know."

"I need to know more about all those golf lessons with Mrs. O'Reilly."

"I've told you—"

"Only that Jones is a good pro."

"Who behaves himself, despite being quite the ladies' man."

"Tell me more."

"I am sorry, Detective. But it's more than one man can handle just to keep this place running. I do not have the time, nor the inclination, to delve into much else."

"Who are you kidding?" I said. "You know when somebody so much as farts around here."

"You and your quaint expressions. I only know that when the members are pleased, I am pleased as well."

Now I've heard everything. But I can play this game better than golf.

"I can tell you run this place like a Swiss clock. You must keep impeccable records."

"Of course."

"Then you must have a copy of Al Jones's résumé on file."

I had pushed one of his buttons. Instead of stonewalling me as usual, he produced the document immediately.

CHAPTER FOURTEEN

Randy Randall escorted me to the front door, saying, "I will make sure it is locked this time." It sounded like he said, Don't let the door hit you in the ass on the way out.

"Is the pro shop open?" I asked.

"It is also closed on Mondays," Randall said.

"Can you let me in?"

"I suppose I could. It *is* my shop, you know. Al Jones merely owns the merchandise."

"Let's go," I said.

"We don't have to go outside," said Randall. "Follow me."

He led me into a passageway off the main entrance hall, past Dame Winifred's provocative portrait.

"It is my shop," he continued, "but Jones makes a fortune from it. I should raise his rent."

The passageway ended with a dark wooden door and a brass plaque engraved Men's Grill.

"Through here . . ." Randall opened the door.

We entered a wood-paneled room filled with sturdy chairs, tables with tidy place settings, a well-stocked bar, and a big-screen TV. Everything any man ever needed.

"I may have to lock this room from now on, too," Randall grumbled. "My liquor has been disappearing."

"You wouldn't want to lose the TV," I said.

"This Brobdingnagian boob tube?" said Randall. "I would not mind in the least. What a pity no one reads anymore."

He opened another dark wooden door, leading me into the men's locker room. I admired the mahogany lockers and wall-to-wall carpet, muttering, "Pretty fancy."

"We do our best," Randall said.

"Is every member's name engraved on his locker in brass?"

"Most assuredly."

"O'Reilly?"

"Of course."

Why didn't I think of it sooner? Bad mistake. Assigned lockers never dawned on me.

"Can you unlock it?"

"No one locks them," Randall said smugly. "Our members are above pilfering."

"How about murder?"

He smirked again, leading me to O'Reilly's locker. I opened it with a ballpoint, careful not to smudge any fingerprints, and found it empty.

"Where's all his stuff?" I said.

"He must have cleaned it out."

"Maybe someone did it for him." Why didn't I think of this yesterday? I should give myself the good old wham-bam.

"It wasn't me, Detective."

"Does Al Jones have a locker?"

Randall led me through a maze of lockers into a cul-de-sac. As I opened Jones's locker with my trusty ballpoint, I quipped, "Besides knowing when anyone farts around here, you know where they hang their jockstraps."

Randall ignored me.

"I can't believe no one locks these things," I added. "Someone stole my old shower shoes at a public course. I can't say pilfered. It was a great loss. All of seventy-nine cents, plus tax. Not including sentimental value, of course."

"How tragic, Detective." Randall forced a smile. No sense of humor, obviously.

"There's nothing but a towel," I said, staring into the pro's locker, "and a pair of golf shoes."

I picked up a shoe, touching only the insides, and turned it over.

"What would one expect in a golf pro's locker?" asked Randall, smartly.

"A spike on the right heel's missing," I observed.

"Spikes come off all the time," Randall shrugged.

"It depends on which spike." I was thinking about the footprint out by the water hazard.

"Ah, you detectives. My aunt was right. Always using your little gray cells," Randall lisped. "Anything else?"

"Next to nothing in Jones's and zilch in O'Reilly's."

"Look at these . . ." I opened several other lockers. They were loaded with stuff, like a shopper's closet.

"What do you think it means?"

"It means I'm taking these golf shoes," I said. "You'll get a property slip."

"I think it's meaningless," Randall said. "Our golf pro did not murder anyone, nor did any of our members. You are wasting the taxpayers' money."

"Cops also pay taxes," I said. "My weekly check takes a worse hit than O'Reilly suffered. Don't touch anything in here," I told him. "I'm sending forensics. And don't worry. They won't pilfer anything. All they'll take are fingerprints."

CHAPTER FIFTEEN

I drove to the Dunkin' Donuts in nearby Glen Cove for a good cup of coffee and a good look at Al Jones's résumé. I also had a croissant, about as continental as I ever get. I would never order a Dunkaccino. I rarely drink anything imported, except a beer called Golfer's Choice occasionally. It comes from Germany, with an old-time golfer on the can, plus a ceramic cap to reseal it. As if any thirsty golfer or self-respecting beer drinker wouldn't kill the whole thing in one sitting.

Jones had been a pro at dozens of country clubs from New York to Texas, if his résumé's not faked. We'll contact the club managers to verify it. Who knows what will turn up? Too many employers, even fastidious types like Randy Randall, fail to do background checks or ignore them. It's odd how some folks are so trusting of everyone but cops.

I had studied Jones's appointment book back in the pro shop. Mrs. O'Reilly was penciled in for lessons almost every day. As the weeks went on, her name became more and more abbreviated. From Mrs. O'Reilly to Mrs. O'R, and

Mrs. O to just plain O. Does the latter stand for orgasm? Does the condom from the sand trap belong to Jones? It is a magnum. Mrs. O's husband is ruled out, for his wicked case of the Irish curse, but a big guy like Jones could be her Texas longhorn.

Jones is not shy. His casual assumption that Mr. O'Reilly was working on his night moves when he got whacked leads me to believe that he could have been humping any one of his lessons out on the course. Then Mr. O happened along and threatened to get him fired, so Jones whacked him. Or Mrs. O could have put him up to it. It seemed to fit, except for Jones being right-handed. Mr. O was definitely done in by a southpaw.

Jones's résumé also indicated that he played major league baseball, one season with the Texas Rangers, before becoming a golf pro. I could verify that information about a mile down the road.

Mike's B.C. × 2 (Batting Cages and Baseball Cards) was a seedy little store in a small shopping center along Sea Cliff Avenue in Glen Cove. Dead last in a row of hodgepodge-ethnic, struggling strip-mall stores: a Korean supermarket, a Jewish deli, an African American dry cleaner, a Chinese takeout, a vacancy where a Pakistani stationer had suddenly left town.

Mike's place reminded me of pre-Rudy Times Square porno shops. Mike was always sitting by the front window, hawking baseball cards as if they were skin mags, dispensing quarters for his beat-up batting cages in back as if they were triple-X video booths. I once tried hitting back there but struck out more times than a blind man waving a Wiffle bat. I insisted the lighting was too dim. Mike laughed and told me the eyes were always first to go.

"Hey, paisan," Mike said, as I entered. "Long time no see. Where you been hiding?"

"Over at Broken Oak," I said.

"Doin' what? Takin' out the garbage?"

"Playing golf."

"Yeah, right." Mike scoffed. "Playin' with yourself, maybe."

We laughed. Mike was an ex-cop, tossed off the force for using too much of the good old wham-bam on a C.W. Post student who attacked him as he tried to break up a bar fight. The firing was a crock, and the community lost a good cop. The kid dropped out of Crayola U and became a crack dealer. Mike came to this. We go back a long way, starting out together as lowly patrolmen, busting crackheads like the so-called student who ended his career. Shaking the doorknobs of dumps like Mike's B.C. × 2 in the middle of the night.

"Where you really been?" Mike asked. "Out at Crab Meadow, over at Eisenhower Park? Still got that golf jones?"

"I told you, at Broken Oak."

"You gotta be kiddin'. They wouldn't let you in the gate, let alone golf there."

"I wasn't golfing, but I can wish."

"You got a sunburn."

"You should try it. You look like shit."

"Rough night." Mike shrugged. "You've had a few of those."

"No more. I've taken up reading."

"Arrest reports?"

"Murder mysteries."

"With all due respect to your wife's memory," Mike said softly, "you need a woman."

"You need customers," I said.

"It's early," said Mike.

"Very funny. But I got a murder at Broken Oak."

I described the goings-on, which had yet to hit the news. I also showed him the résumé.

He scanned it and said, "You got any idea how many rookies come and go in one season in a club like the Rangers? In and out of high school, college, the minors. On and off injuries, drugs, the sauce. It's a revolving door, like our criminal justice system. I never hearda this guy. Unless he's Mark McGuire, even his rookie card is worthless. Kinda like rookie cops. But for you, paisan, I'll look through my big book. If this guy's got a card, it'll be in here."

Mike flipped through a fat, dog-eared reference book. Stopping suddenly, running a thick finger down one of the pages.

"Could this be it?" he said, pointing at a name.

"Jones, Thomas Alva," I read, squinting at the tiny print. "Texas Rangers 1985."

"It's gotta be," said Mike.

"It only says Al on his résumé," I said.

"Isn't Alva a girl's name?"

"Ever heard of Thomas Alva Edison?"

"Who'd he play for?"

"Come on, Mike. Got his card?"

"For you, my half-Polack paisan, I'll even look through my big box."

"You're all heart, you big guinea."

"Hey. I'm doin' you a favor here."

Mike pulled a large cardboard box filled with baseball cards from under a counter. I collected cards as a kid. Had a few that would be worth a fortune these days. But my mom, like everyone else's, threw them out.

"Got it," Mike finally said. "Right here in the rookie section."

He pulled out a card, examined it briefly, and muttered, "No wonder he never made it. He was an Interstate hitter. I-40 equals a .140 batting average. It's an old baseball joke. Yours would be even less."

Ignoring that last comment, I looked at the card. On the front was a young, lanky-looking Al Jones. On back was only a single line of stats.

"Jesus, Mary, and Joseph," I whispered.

"Even they can't help Interstate hitters," Mike said.

"I didn't mean that. He batted left and right, a switch hitter."

"No shit, Sherlock. He sucked from both sides. He was also stupid, using an alias like Al. Even you could figure that out."

I gave him the finger.

"Watch out," Mike warned. "Some shyster'll throw Alva in your face when you go to trial. Claiming the murder was his parents' fault for giving him a girl's name."

CHAPTER SIXTEEN

I dropped the golf shoes from Al Jones's locker at the forensics lab. It would take some time to examine them. Too much time, if you ask me. I know, nobody asked. But lab techs do not have the same sense of urgency as the average tec, though homicides should be solved posthaste. If killers are not caught within forty-eight hours, the odds against finding them become astronomical.

On my way back to Bayville, I wondered if the missing spike would be enough for a conviction. Even if it matches the heel print by the water hazard, it does not place Jones there when the murder occurred. Being a switch-hitter won't convict him, either. I need a motive. There are no murders without motives. The motive for O'Reilly's murder must lay, so to speak, with his wife and Al Jones.

I need some hard evidence, no pun intended. There's nothing yet, nothing with enough substance to scare the suspects and somehow trip them up. Rendering tried-and-true detective's handbook methods useless. Sure, I can play one suspect against the other. I can also recruit a fellow tec for good cop/bad cop. But Mrs. O is sharp as a tack, and

Jones is smarter than his good-ole-boy exterior indicates. There's a plenitude of little gray cells between them, as Dame Winifred Randall's Couloir might observe, and their alibis are in alignment. I need something unusual to unmask them. Something beyond the detective's handbook, but short of the good old wham-bam. Something needs to happen. "'Tis here but yet confused," my higher-educated wife might have put it, "knavery's plain face is never seen 'til used." She was full of Shakespeare quotes, and occasionally full of herself, God forgive me.

I got home at 6:00 P.M., late for some working people, not late enough for someone living alone. There's too much daylight left in the summer. I noticed that my lawn needed cutting and my house needed painting. Most of all, I needed a drink.

I parked beside my tenants' car, pleased they were home in their upstairs apartment. Their creaking floorboards and muffled conversations were the next best thing to a companion of my own. I wished they were my kids.

I grabbed the mail on my way to the kitchen. There were scads of bills, something serious-looking from the PBA, what felt like five pounds of advertising fliers, and the local mullet wrapper, with a breaking front-page story on the murder at Broken Oak Country Club.

I tossed everything onto a kitchen counter and frisked the fridge for a cold one. Horror of horrors, no brewskis. I deserve at least one; the day's been long and hot. I've also got a good excuse to celebrate, being on the cusp of collaring Al Jones. I guess I can wait, for the beer and the bust. I'm also waiting for the lab work on his shoes, for the guys in the white coats with all the gizmos. Though I'd rather go for the gusto and bust Jones right now. It has to be his heel print by O'Reilly's body. He had to be there with a five iron, swinging it southpaw like a baseball bat. Rookie cards don't lie. He also had to be boinking Mrs. O. Why wait for DNA on the panties and in the condom from the bunker, when lab techs have a bunker mentality? What's forensics compared to gut feelings? What gas chromatic mass spectrometer can determine if Jones had acted on his own or if Mrs. O put him up to it? Why not bust him right now? DNA? A fig. Just give me a few minutes alone with that tall Texan in a backroom at headquarters. Sure, Kanopka. Then you can bend over and kiss your butt, plus your career, good-bye.

I found a warm Bud behind the toaster oven, stuffed it into the freezer, and went to my bedroom. Watched beer never chills. But what to do in the interim? I noticed Dame Winifred's little paperback lying helpless and exposed on my night table, like O'Reilly's open fly by the water hazard. Now that I know it's *Murder on the Moor*, according to Randy Randall, will I like it any better? I sat on my bed and began reading.

The little book was oddly becoming comfortable, like one of my regular snitches. It was also oddly like O'Reilly's murder, though I did not expect to find any useful insights. An old biddie with a rusty Smith-Corona can't compare with twenty years of busting felons with my trusty Smith & Wesson.

A few more pages fell out. I slipped them back in. They did not fit quite right, like an old deck of cards that can't stack straight and even. Reading on, I learned that the gun-loving earl of Cranbrook was more concerned about his grouse hunt than about the corpse out on his moor. Like Dr. Fitch being more concerned about getting in a round of golf than about O'Reilly?

A butler was also lurking. Like Randy Randall? Plus the gamekeeper who found the body out on the moor with a bullet hole in its back, like Vince Henry, the black greenskeeper at Broken Oak who found O'Reilly? Other odd help, like Slim and his cadre caddies, also crept in and out. And the murdered guy on the moor was nearly as obnoxious as O'Reilly. Despite the similarities, however, I had nothing in common with Detective Peter H. Couloir and his little gray cells.

In the next chapter, Dame Winifred introduced two new characters. Mrs. Phelps was the victim's wife, a renowned concert pianist and most attractive. She reminded me of Mrs. O and was most likely messing around with the next new character, Algernon Spotswood, a fun-loving sportsman, aka Algie, a frequent guest at the earl's estate. Algie was grouse hunting with the earl prior to Mr. Phelps's body being discovered. He could easily have copped the Webley-Vickers .44 from the earl's arms collection and done the dastardly deed.

Algie also reminded me of Al Jones and pond scum. *Murder on the Moor* had more red herrings than a Sheepshead Bay fishmonger. All of them slowed up the story. I'm used to cutting to the chase.

Dame Winifred gave Algie an alibi. *"I arrived here only this morning,"* he said, *"well after this unfortunate incident. And I do understand that the poor chap was shot quite some time ago."*

I stopped reading a moment, wondering if Al Jones and Mrs. O were together right now. Perfecting their alibis? Performing carnal acts? Should I put a tail on them? Was the murder planned in advance? Had Jones seized the moment? Encountering O'Reilly hopelessly drunk, helplessly peeing into the water hazard? Where's the five iron with ashes on its blade and, as Peter H. Couloir would say, a soupçon of O'Reilly's blood? In fact, he's questioning Algie about the murder weapon on the next page.

"*You are an expert with firearms?*" Couloir asked.

"*Quite, Detective. From my experiences as a military officer, champion skeet shooter, and hunter.*"

"*Are these weapons of destruction all rifles, monsieur?*"

"*And pistols, of course. But I resent your implication that they are weapons of wanton destruction. I use them only for targets and humane, well-regulated hunting. It's called sport, old man.*"

Way to go, Couloir. Algie sounds like a charter member of the NRA. Piss him off some more. You've been too polite so far. Pissing off suspects is one of my favorite pastimes, my most successful method for making them tip their hand. I wonder how far I can go with Al Jones before he grabs a shiny new iron from one of his display racks and swings it at my cranium. Can I duck quickly enough? My reflexes ain't what they used to be.

"*And you are familiar with the Webley-Vickers quarante-quatre?*" Couloir went on.

"*The .44?*"

"*Mais oui.*"

I suddenly like Couloir's lapsing into French, further trying Algie's patience. I also approve of his testing Algie's knowledge of the murder weapon. He seems more familiar with guns than he lets on.

"*An extremely powerful hand gun, Detective. Standard military issue, for officers, you know.*"

"*You were a guest of the Earl when his Webley-Vickers was removed from its display case?*"

"*What are you implying?*"

"*I imply nothing, monsieur. I am merely setting the time frame, and putting my facts in their proper order.*"

End of chapter? I flipped the page to make certain. How could it end with Couloir backing down? He may have been a good detective in his day, but that was then and this is now. The only thing we have in common is no female companionship. But I'm not sure he misses it. Despite his heavy gray matter, he seems a little light in the loafers.

I wonder if my Bud's gotten cold. I need some beer in my belly as well as sizzle in my synapses.

CHAPTER SEVENTEEN

Tuesday morning I was wide awake at the crack of dawn, excited about getting to forensics and getting the goods on Al Jones. Having dreamed that his golf shoes, with the missing heel spike, matched the heel print by O'Reilly's body, I figured dreams about murder are not always nightmares. I hopped out of bed, showered, shaved, pulled on some clothes. Then I hurried outside to my car and drove to the Glen Cove Dunkin' Donuts for some coffee and an oat bran muffin. I don't like making arrests on an empty stomach.

The forensics lab was open when I arrived. The techs were excited and extremely pleased with themselves. My dream had come true. The shoe with the missing spike matched the print by the water hazard exactly. They also found traces of ash in the seams between the soles and the uppers of both shoes. The same kind of ash in O'Reilly's head wound, from the blade of the five iron.

"What's the source of this stuff?" I asked the head tech.

"A fire," he shrugged. "What else?"

I said patiently, "I already know that ashes come from burning something."

"Probably a campfire," the tech continued. "There's wood, paper, traces of tallow."

"Tallow?"

"Animal fat. From a hamburger, maybe."

"Oh, I get it," I said. "They were having a barbecue, and the killer is a Campfire Girl."

The tech shrugged again and said, "Possibility. But this is more like fast food. Maybe a Big Mac."

"Great," I said sarcastically. "What good are these electron microscopes and molecular measuring devices, or whatever you use, most likely a ginsu knife and a veal mallet, when they diminish matter, and my evidence, to such an elemental state that I can't see the woods for the trees?"

"That doesn't matter," the lab tech said. "Fact is, these elements are inextricably linked."

I paused a moment, giving my woefully weak little gray cells a chance to catch up, then said, "You mean the ashes on the five iron and the ashes on the shoes, plus the heel print at the site of the murder, will get me a conviction?"

"If you know who was wearing the shoes."

"Great," I said, meaning it this time.

CHAPTER EIGHTEEN

I drove immediately to Broken Oak to arrest Al Jones. Though I believed I could still handle a man Jones's size by myself, I'm only five-ten and he's got six inches on me. I brought along another detective and a uniformed cop as a backup.

"That's Jones's Crown Vic," I told them, parking near a large sedan in the lot closest to the clubhouse.

"Looks like a state trooper's car," said Vinnie Donnelly, the other detective, who's spent seventeen years working homicide and would kill to play golf here.

"I'd stop him in a heartbeat," growled the uniform, named Mickey Roche, who used to chase speeders on the Grand Central Parkway. "Those Texas plates stand out like a sore thumb."

"Take it easy," I told Mickey. "You're not on your Harley."

"This guy's also armed and dangerous," Vinnie reminded us, though we only knew about the five iron.

"He's lucky we're not bustin' him in the Lone Star State," Mickey said, as we climbed out of my car. "They got the death penalty there and they use it."

"They should execute some of these cars," said Vinnie. "I thought these people had big bucks. Look at that crummy, dirty, banged-up Yugo."

"The beaters belong to the staff," I told him.

"How do you know?"

"It's too early for most of the members," I said, wondering if Dr. Fitch was out on dawn patrol.

"And the course looks empty," Mickey added.

"Good thinking," Vinnie told him. "You might make detective, someday."

"What makes you think I'd want to?" Mickey growled. "Your pay and your rank's no better than mine."

"Our hours are shittier," Vinnie said.

"Okay," said Mickey. "I'll give you that."

"Wait near the car," I ordered, still head detective on this case.

They both nodded.

"I'll go into the pro shop," I continued. "If I'm not out in five minutes, come and get me. But watch out for a tall Texan with a five iron."

"Or a smoking hog leg?"

"Yeah. That, too."

I followed a cart path past the first tee and practice putting green. The summer sun was rising peacefully, birds were chirping. Wisps of night mist lingered in vales along the verdant fairways. Don't get distracted, I warned myself. Al Jones could be lurking in the larkspur. *Lurking in the Larkspur*? Sounds like the title of a Dame Winifred mystery.

The door to the pro shop was slightly ajar. I opened it wider, ever so slowly, hesitating before stepping inside. It was too quiet and too dark. I stood perfectly still, hoping to hear someone moving, to feel the presence, with infinitesimal airflow, or something metaphysical. The Force be with me. Something told me someone was in there.

Stepping quickly and quietly inside, I closed the door behind me. Too many cops make targets of themselves in open door frames. I found a light switch but left it off. My antennae were out and my hackles were up. Goosebumps and gut feelings were needed more than little gray cells now that Jones could be hiding behind a counter or a clothing rack, gripping his five iron.

I gripped my .38 snub-nose, which feels even better than a five iron. Unless I'm hitting about 150 yards to the green.

There were too many hiding places. I slipped past some shelves loaded with pastel cotton sweaters and argyle socks. I would not mind having a few of the items in my golf wardrobe, though I *would* mind dressing better than I play. I scolded myself for thinking about clothes and my golf game. The older you get, the tougher it gets to stay focused.

I focused on two tall racks of women's clothing that could be a gauntlet for the good-ole-boy golf pro. He could easily leap out, five iron flashing, bludgeon my aging cranium and the few gray cells left, slip outside past my backup, and hightail it out of town.

I heard a muffled sound from a stockroom in back. I slipped between the two tall clothing racks, thankfully not getting whacked. I sidled toward the stockroom door, with Smith & Wesson leading the way.

I know that Jones is in the stockroom, but he may not know that I'm in the shop. He's making too much noise. I breathed a soft sigh of relief, believing that surprise was in my favor. Until I cocked my pistol and kicked in the stockroom door, shouting, "Freeze!"

"Christ!" Randy Randall clutched his chest.

"Where's Al Jones?" I snapped, hoping I had not given Randall a heart attack.

"I-I haven't seen him . . ." Randall's voice went up at least an octave, as if I were squeezing my trigger and his scrotum.

"What are you doing in here?" I demanded.

"I own this shop," Randall said, testily. Recovering his composure too damn quickly, along with his snotty attitude.

"So you've told me," I said. "But your golf pro's guilty of murder and I'm arresting him."

"I haven't seen him this morning," Randall said. "Please put that pistol away."

I grudgingly lowered my snub-nose. Why is it cops who always get handcuffed? Forget it, Kanopka. The killer's escaping. This is not the time for police-related polemics.

"Stay here," I told Randall. "My backup will be in any minute. I hope they don't mistake you for Jones."

I darted to the front door and shouted outside to Vinnie and Mickey, already on their way up the cart path, "It's Kanopka! Jones is loose! Call for more backup! Search the grounds!"

I went back to Randall, who was still in the stockroom, and told him, "Wait outside in front."

"I can't," he insisted.

"Why not?"

"You need me. Are you searching the mansion?"

"You bet."

"It's a maze of dark hallways and a myriad of anterooms."

"So?"

"With secret passages, false panels, concealed closets, and pocket doors."

"So what?"

"Al Jones knows some of the hiding places," Randall said, "but I know them all."

I realized that he was right.

"You can stay with me," I said, "but *behind* me."

Randall followed me through the side door from the pro shop into the men's locker room.

"How many other ways out of here?" I asked.

"Only one," he told me. "Through the main house. If he opens any windows, an alarm will go off."

I quickly but cautiously checked the showers, toilets, sauna, janitor's closet, culs-de-sac formed by the fancy wooden lockers, pleased that Randall was guiding me through the labyrinthine layout but annoyed that Al Jones was nowhere to be found.

We entered the main house.

"Ever get lost in here?" I asked.

"Sometimes," said Randall, guiding me swiftly through the kitchen, past Garland stoves with umpteen burners into a pantry that would make Emeril envious and a walk-in freezer the size of an Iron Chef's ego. Still no Jones poised to lambaste me with a frozen leg of lamb.

Moving on, through the men's grill and the main dining room, we entered a lounge filled with art deco sofas and chairs, clustered around chic little cocktail tables. There was also a long, low bar that could easily have concealed the culprit armed with an ice pick, a cocktail shaker, or a longneck beer bottle. I could use a long-neck right now.

"He could be anywhere," Randall said, glancing nervously around.

"Scared?" I asked.

"A little," he admitted.

"What's behind that big curtain over there?"

"The arras?"

"Yeah. That one."

"Perhaps we'll find Polonius," Randall said theatrically, trying not to betray his stage fright.

"Stay back . . ." I said, throwing aside the curtain, arras if you must, finding only bare walls. I got the sinking feeling that Jones had vanished.

We headed upstairs but stopped as pounding sounds echoed from the main entrance hall.

"Sounds like a pile driver," I said.

"Someone's at the front door," said Randall.

Hope it's Houdini, I thought, to help me find Jones.

I cracked the massive front door and called out, to a phalanx of uniformed cops, "It's Kanopka! We're the good guys! But our killer's still loose!"

I deployed all the cops, half onto the golf course and grounds and the other half into the house.

"Let's hit the upper floors," I told Randall. "I don't like basements."

"Why not?" he asked.

"Must be the old Polish joke about trying to commit suicide by jumping out a basement window."

Moving rapidly through the maze of upstairs rooms, I posted uniformed cops in strategic corridors and stairwells, so our culprit couldn't slip behind us, or hide where we'd already searched and escape later.

Randall and I stopped at a thick Gothic door sealed with burglar bars and heavy padlocks at the end of a dark corridor.

"Where does this lead?" I asked.

"To a stairway," said Randall.

"A stairway to heaven?"

"Just another room."

"Open it."

"Why? You can see by the way it's locked, no one could have entered. Besides, I don't have the keys."

"Get them."

"I don't know where they are."

"No problem. I'll get a crowbar."

"But there's nothing up there," Randall insisted, blocking the door with his body. "And the door is very old, all hand-carved. You'll ruin it."

"That's your problem. Mine is that the killer could be in there."

I was about to call for a crowbar when I heard my name being shouted up a back stairwell. I dashed downstairs, leaving Randall and his cherished door alone for the moment, and found two uniforms with Slim the caddy.

"This guy says he saw Al Jones running across the golf course," one of the uniforms told me.

"When?" I asked.

"'Bout an hour ago," said Slim, grinning and displaying his rotten teeth. His breath smelled like cheap wine of unknown vintage. Why does Randy Randall allow him on the grounds? Is he that good a caddy?

"Which way was he headed?" I asked.

"I already told them." Slim nodded at the uniforms, weaving slightly.

"Now tell me . . ." I drew close and stared at him, hoping the visceral challenge would elicit quicker answers and his breath wouldn't bowl me over.

"Out past the tenth tee," he continued, grinning. His B.O. was also brutal.

"We checked that direction," someone else said. "There's a fence around the course's perimeter, but plenty of places where you can slip through or climb over."

"Issue an alert," I ordered. "Cover the trains, boats, planes, and don't forget MacArthur Airport. Also check the rental car companies and bus stations. Go beyond the usual. I want this guy."

"Do I get a reward?" Slim asked.

"We'll see," I said.

We have to catch Al Jones first, and the odds are becoming slim to none.

CHAPTER NINETEEN

I raced to O'Reilly's house. Jones could be hiding there, though most felons try to get as far away as possible. Mrs. O opened the front door before I could ring the bell. This time she was dressed.

"May I help you?" she asked, like I'm a stranger asking for directions.

"Where's Al Jones?" I snapped.

"Do you need golf lessons?"

"He murdered your husband."

"What's that got to do with me?"

"You were having an affair with him."

"I was only taking golf lessons."

She looked genuinely annoyed. A damn good actress.

"Then you won't mind me looking around," I said.

"You and who else?" She glanced behind me down the driveway. Like I need help. Like Jones is hiding behind the door with his five iron ready to brain me?

"I'm all it takes," I said, reaching for my snub-nose.

"You and a search warrant," she said, eyes narrowing.

I liked her feistiness. It reminded me of Carol. Once she told me I'd need a body cast if I ever forgot our wedding anniversary again.

"I don't need a warrant when—"

"I know," she interrupted. "There's probable cause, or some such legalese, that gives you the right to run rampant through my house. Go ahead and look, if it makes you happy."

I stepped cautiously inside, liking her dislike of legalese, wary of Jones leaping out at me. He was not behind the door, however, or in the front hall closet. Mrs. O followed as I went through the house.

"Would you like some coffee?" she asked, in the kitchen.

"Where does this go?"

"My bedroom. By the way, Al Jones has never been there."

"Then why did you call him the day after your husband was murdered?"

"How do you know?"

"Your cell phone told me. Out by the pool, when you loaned it to me. I hit the redial button, and guess who answered?"

Dame Winifred would love the technological twist. It could inspire a mystery in itself. Maybe *Murder and Ma Bell*. There is a ring to it, but what's in a title? My wife was always telling me a book needs sentences, chapters and some other stuff.

"I should charge you for the call," Mrs. O said, following me out of the kitchen.

"Should I charge you with the murder?" I countered.

"I hate to burst your bubble," she told me, "but I was only canceling a golf lesson."

"Your lover would charge you for a no-show?"

"Not likely, is it?"

"I have the receipts."

"That would prove we're not lovers, wouldn't it?"

"It's also good cover."

Nothing in her bedroom, but I countered, "If my spouse was just murdered, my last concern would be canceling a golf lesson."

"Don't believe it," said Mrs. O. "It's amazing what comes to mind in times of grief."

She was right. I must have accomplished at least a few mundane tasks the day Carol died, though I can't recall anything but abject grief.

"By your own admission," I said, "you weren't grieving."

"Come on, Detective. You know what I mean."

"You know that you have the right to remain silent?"

"You arresting me?"

"Not yet."

"What does that mean?"

"It'll go a lot easier if you tell me everything you know."

"That I conspired with my golf pro to kill my husband? Come on, Detective. You've been watching too many cop shows."

"I don't watch cop shows."

"Then reading too many mystery novels."

Hmm.

"Did you put Al Jones up to it?"

"No," she answered evenly.

"And he's not here?"

"He has never been here."

"That's not the answer."

"Okay, Detective. Al Jones *is not here.*"

For some strange reason I believed her.

"You've seen everything," she said.

"So I have," I said, visions of her swimming stark-naked dancing in my head. "Do you know where he is?"

"Get this straight, Detective. I'm not his lover, his mistress, his murder accomplice, or his keeper."

I detected disdain for the tall Texan, which could even have fooled the exceedingly skeptical Peter H. Couloir, though Mrs. O's great tits and beguiling smile would have had no impact on the limp-wristed little tec.

"When we get him," I assured Mrs. O, "and we will get him, *he* won't be so protective."

She laughed, but I didn't take offense. I was being melodramatic. And the thought never crossed my mind, though it would with any other suspect who laughed at me, to give her a chip shot in some sensitive area for showing disrespect.

"Let us know where Jones is hiding," I simply said, "and we'll cut you some slack at the sentencing."

She laughed again. I liked the sound. It was almost like Carol.

CHAPTER TWENTY

Midnight in the Broken Oak parking lot overlooking the garden of good and evil: glorious golf and murder most foul. In deep shadows in my unmarked car, I was parked across the lot from Al Jones's car. Staring like an owl stalking a rabbit, ready to pounce if Jones came back. Coming back for the big Crown Vic with Texas plates seemed even a longer shot than his showing up earlier at Mrs. O'Reilly's, but I was desperate. We had no trace of him.

If he made it to Manhattan, where a tall Texan swinging a bloody five iron along Ninth Avenue could be considered normal, the crush of inhumanity could hide him forever. If he stole a car, he could be in Texas by now. No one pays stolen cars any attention. My only hope is *America's Most Wanted*.

Stranger things have happened than Jones coming back for his ride, however. Criminals can get pretty stupid. And someone else might show. Like Mrs. O, trying somehow to help her lover. I'd normally tow the car immediately to the lab and let forensics go through it, but I decided to leave it untouched until the next day. I had to try something different. I was desperate. I was also in trouble at headquarters for not using more backup when I first came to make the arrest. The brass informed me, after the fact of course, that I should have flooded the joint with blue uniforms. Hindsight at headquarters is always 20-20.

I sat alone in the parking lot for hours, hoping for a call on my short wave that would help the investigation, surfing between talk shows and music stations on my AM/FM, wondering why rappers, punk rockers, and talk show callers are so full of hate, wishing I had brought one of my Chuck Berry CDs and that my unmarked car had a player. WFAN was broadcasting a baseball game, but it was a blowout. And the New York Inevitables, aka the Yankees, would make the playoffs anyway.

I had read two newspapers from cover to cover and finished both crosswords. The *New York Times* was easy. I do them every day except Sunday. I used to do the Sunday puzzle with Carol, when I wasn't playing golf. She knew words like *Erse* and *esne*, I knew words like *Spahn* and *Sain*. What to do now, at midnight in the garden of golf and grisly murder? Another good title for a Dame Winifred mystery? Which reminded me, I had brought *Murder on the Moor* with me. But I was afraid to start reading it in case it put me asleep. If Al Jones sneaked back and managed to escape in his own car, headquarters would justifiably have my hide.

I removed the yellowed and broken little paperback from my glove compartment, along with a penlight, and opened it carefully so as not to lose any more pages. I had stopped at a good part. The arrogant, gun-loving Algernon Spotswood, aka Algie or murdering pond scum, like Al Jones, is about to get his comeuppance. Algie is escaping on the Orient Express, which is just pulling out of the Gare du

Nord in Paris, as Dame Winifred's Peter H. Couloir hops on board. I was not sure how Couloir and Algie had gotten to this point, as several pages prior were missing, but I got the main drift.

Couloir bustled down the narrow corridor of the sleeping car, squeezing past confused passengers, whispering, "Pardon . . . pardon . . ." until he stopped at Algernon Spotswood's closed compartment door . . .

Hope he breaks it down and coldcocks the son of a bitch.

Couloir tapped lightly . . .

Limp-wristed wimp.

. . . calling out, "Porter, si vous plait" . . .

I like that. Once I posed as a pizza delivery man to catch a killer.

. . . but there was no answer . . .

Crap.

. . . tried the door, and found it unlocked . . .

Watch out!

. . . compartment was completely empty . . .

What now? The next two pages were missing. I jumped ahead.

. . . in the baggage car, Couloir spied Algernon Spotswood's steamer trunk . . .

Hmm.

. . . and deftly picked the latch . . . threw open the lid . . . stood back . . . and gasped . . . Spotswood's body was curled inside . . . in the fetal position . . . stone dead . . .

The prime suspect dead in his own steamer trunk on the Orient Express? What claptrap. That would be like Al Jones shipping himself out on the auto/train to Disney World.

I stuffed the little book back into my glove compartment, stretched, yawned, longed for some hot coffee, hoped to stay awake for the duration. Somewhere in the wee hours I would have to call for relief.

A thick night mist wafted into the parking lot, shrouding Jones's car. I could barely see it. What if the big Crown Vic disappears into the mist, like a David Copperfield illusion? Stop thinking like that, Kanopka. Letting your life become illusory since your wife lost hers. Evanescence, she would have termed it, and worried about my melancholy. If Jones's car disappeared in the mist, however, I'd get an instant reality check in the form of an ass-reaming at headquarters. I shivered at the thought and at the sudden realization that, in all the hustle and bustle, I had taken only a cursory look at the car. Peter H. Couloir would surely have popped the trunk, as he had on the Orient Express. What was I thinking?

I hopped out of my car, removed the tire iron from its trunk, and stalked toward the Crown Vic, like Jones stalking O'Reilly with the five iron.

Cutting through the mist, across the fifty yards of tarmac toward the big sedan from the Lone Star State, seemed surreal. My heart was beating like a trip-hammer and my footsteps echoed like thunder, blowing my state of mind and my stakeout. Betraying my presence and botching this case to every cop and the entire criminal world. What if the murder weapon's in the trunk? Why hadn't I thought of that before? Headquarters will kick me from here to kingdom come. What if it's even worse? Like another murder victim. Like Algernon Spotswood's body in that steamer trunk on the Orient Express? Or body parts, and good ole boy Al Jones is a serial killer?

Inserting the tire iron into a crevice, I popped the Crown Vic's cavernous trunk. Though the trunk light was dim and wisps of night mist further diffused it, I could easily tell the body inside belonged to Al Jones.

CHAPTER TWENTY-ONE

Forensics pecked at the Crown Vic like corbies on road-kill, while two pontificating captains pecked at me.

"Wicked head wound," said Captain Gleason, staring at Jones, still in the trunk.

"Another golf club," Captain Kowalski declared.

"You think?" I smirked. Kowalski's a ball buster like Gleason, but beneath contempt.

"I'd bet a month's salary," Kowalski continued, "the same guy nailed that mick out here by the water hole. And don't cry just because this guy in the trunk was your prime suspect."

"He still is," I said.

"You must be kidding," Kowalski scoffed. "You sure you're only half Polack?"

"I've got the best of both worlds," I told my superiors.

"You got nothin' in this murder case," Kowalski reminded me, as if I needed it.

"We've been following your progress," Gleason added.

"What progress?" Kowalski said, with a shit-eating grin. "He's back to square one."

"You're right," said Gleason. "He needs another suspect, preferably living."

"What makes you so sure that Jones didn't kill O'Reilly?" I asked. "He had motive and opportunity."

"Tell us the motive."

"I'm pretty sure he was sleeping with O'Reilly's wife." Pretty sure? Jesus.

"Can you prove they were getting it on?"

"No."

"Then why are you wasting our time?"

"I mean I can't prove it yet."

"I got it," Kowalski grinned. "Jones felt guilty about killing the mick and committed suicide by whacking himself in the head and locking himself in the trunk."

I always wondered how he made captain. He had to be the inspiration for every Polish joke.

"You're a damn good detective," Gleason said, "but remind me why this stiff was your prime suspect."

"He wanted O'Reilly's wife."

"Wasn't she getting a divorce?" Gleason.

"Yeah. Couldn't he wait?" Kowalski.

"They wanted the life insurance." Gleason.

"They were in it together?" Kowalski.

"That's too obvious." A faint reply from yours truly.

"Plus his property. He's got a hell of a house over on Dosoris." Kowalski again.

"You checked his finances?" Gleason asked.

"We're in the process," I told him.

"What's taking so long?" Kowalski said.

"You know how it goes," I shrugged, though it's up to me to push for quick answers.

"We know all about the bastard." Kowalski grinned like a Cheshire cat. "He was flat broke and borrowed to the max."

"You prick!" I snapped.

"Hey!" Kowalski shot back. "Don't forget, I'm your captain."

"Sorry, Karl," said Gleason. "We should have told you sooner."

"Instead of hoarding it down at headquarters, hanging me out to dry?"

"He said we're sorry." Kowalski continued grinning.

"Sure. What about his life insurance?"

"He didn't have any," Gleason said.

"In fact," said Kowalski, "his wife's gotta come up with some serious coin to keep that house."

"Jones was stupid if he offed him for money," Gleason said.

"Stupider if he did it to get the fucker's wife when she was already getting divorced," Kowalski said.

"You figure she put him up to it?" Gleason asked.

"What else?" Kowalski said, as if he had written the homicide handbook. "She didn't have to let him know her husband was broke."

"I'd have done it if she didn't have two nickels to rub together," I said, flashing back to her bouncing naked on the diving board. I almost said *two nipples*.

"Can you crack her?" Gleason asked.

"Sounds like he'd like to," Kowalski winked at me.

"She's smart and she's tough," I told them, ignoring the innuendo, trying to sound clinical.

"Could she have done this?"

"She could have done this to keep him quiet," Gleason interrupted me, as forensics prepared to lift Jones out of the trunk.

"She could also have done it for revenge," said Kowalski.

"She was divorcing the SOB," I said brightly. "There was no love lost between them."

"Some divorces are amicable."

"So I've heard, along with other urban legends."

"You're a legend in your own mind, Kanopka."

"And you're a protean Polack genius."

"Hey. I'm your—"

"Sorry. You're a protean Polack genius, Captain Kowalski."

"Cut it out, you two," Gleason said. "There's also a heel print at the murder scene that matches Jones's golf shoes."

"So what?" said Kowalski. "There must be a million heel prints out there."

"That's strong stuff." Gleason smacked his lips, as if he'd just downed a shot of Old Bushmills.

"Let me get this straight," said Kowalski. "O'Reilly was murdered out on the golf course, by a water hazard, around midnight, by a guy wearing golf shoes?"

"What are you driving at?" Gleason asked, golf pun unintended.

"Who plays golf in the dark?" Kowalski said.

"Golf pros, caught in the daily routine of lessons, filling out foursomes, running the shop, what have you, often wear their spikes around the clock." I think I smirked at him.

"Like cops always carry their pieces?"

"Precisely," I said. I didn't dare say *précisement*. Anyway, the two captains seemed to accept the analogy.

"The course gets damp at night," I added. "Jones could have been wearing the spikes to make sure of his murder stance."

"Which makes it premeditated," Gleason said.

"That's nice," Kowalski smirked back at me. "Murder in the first. Now we can put him away for life. Oh, I forgot. He's already dead."

Gleason said, "Five iron last time, wasn't it?"

"With ashes on it," I said.

"Ashes?" They both looked surprised.

"From a campfire, or something like that. Forensics found them in the head wound."

We watched forensics lifting the body, curled like an Iron Age corpse in a peat bog.

Gleason nodded, considering my information. Kowalski could not help opening his big yap one more time.

"If this guy's head wound also has ashes," he said, "I bet it's from the same weapon."

"Maybe not," I said.

"Okay. At least it's gotta be the same killer."

"Maybe not."

"Don't be ridiculous. Even the head wound's on the same side. A lefty whacked O'Reilly. Right?"

"Correct."

"Looks like a lefty whacked this guy, too."

"Maybe," I said.

"Another definite maybe?" asked Kowalski. "You should know how these things work. It's the same killer. I'd stake your reputation on it."

"Why you Pecksniffian putz."

"What's that?"

"You don't know what a putz is?"

"Of course. It's that other word. And don't forget—"

"Sorry, Captain."

I'm not sure what Pecksniffian means, but my wife used it occasionally and it sounds pretty bad. I hope it means someone who sniffs peckers.

"You know," Kowalski's eyes narrowed, "we can take you off this case."

"Calm down," Gleason broke in. "I only want to know if it's the same murder weapon."

Before I could answer, a young woman from forensics ventured, "It's quite possible."

The ME, the one I disliked, overheard her, and asked, "You a golfer?"

"No," she admitted.

"Then what do you know about club selection?" he said, with a glare that warned her not to offer any more opinions.

That irked me. I welcome opinions. Even from know-it-alls like Kowalski. It shows confidence, though most often misguided in Kowalski's case. It's like going for the green in one shot over woods or water instead of playing it safe. It's the only way to go when you're cornered. I can also play it safe, the only way this ME plays it. So he's only allowed to work on stiffs and hide behind microscopes. I would have told him so, if I wasn't under the microscope myself.

"There's no blood in the car or in the trunk," said another forensics person, waving a high-powered flashlight.

"Any on the ground?" I asked.

"Not that we've found."

"Which means he was killed somewhere else?"

"Of course," Kowalski said, as if he'd authored the Forensics Manifesto.

"Where?" I asked. "That's the question."

"Out on the golf course, of course," Kowalski shrugged.

"In the mansion?" Gleason said.

"What about O'Reilly's house?" I said.

"You think a woman did this?"

"Why not?"

Mrs. O *could* have whacked Jones, though her golf swing sucked. What irony if, during all those lessons, her eye was on his cranium instead of the ball. But Jones was a big guy, and she might not be strong enough to dump him into the trunk. She could have had some help. But who? And why?

Had she put Jones up to murdering her husband? Was she afraid he'd break down under Kowalski's clever questioning? I'll have to wait again for forensics. For the approximate time of death, possible location, probable murder weapon. All definite maybes. I'd better not tell Kowalski.

"A guy that size looks odd in the fetal position," I said, as they loaded Jones into the meat wagon.

"You finished with his car?" Gleason asked someone else from forensics, as they tidied up.

"Not by a long shot. We're taking it back to the lab."

"Bet it's the same killer," Kowalski repeated, like a broken record.

"Still my case?" I asked Gleason, without expression.

To my surprise, Kowalski answered, emphatically, "Of course it is."

Maybe he's not such a doofus. Or maybe he just can't wait to watch me fall flat on my face.

"By the way," Gleason asked, "what made you look in the trunk?"

Well, you see, I was sitting out here in the parking lot, reading an old paperback. No. I'd never admit that. Nor would I admit that *Murder on the Moor* had prompted me, that Algernon Spotswood's body in a steamer trunk on the Orient Express got me off my duff. They'd think I was crazy and take me off the case. Sorry, Dame Winifred.

"Just a hunch," I answered.

CHAPTER TWENTY-TWO

At 3:00 A.M. everyone was gone, along with Al Jones's body in the meat wagon and his Crown Vic. I stood alone in the empty parking lot, pondering murder in the dark. Not the Broken Oak murders, but *Murder on the Moor.* Damn that dated little tome. Its title kept running through my mind. Visions of Algernon Spotswood stuffed in a steamer trunk on the Orient Express kept flashing before my eyes like a slide show. I should toss it into the nearest trash can, give myself the good old wham-bam for wasting time, and get back to reality.

I finally climbed into my car, the obstacle of my prime suspect having been whacked. I was feeling like a new golfer who's been forced to play Bethpage Black, though his best drive carries only 150 yards and you need at least 200 to make most of the fairways.

Instead of heading home to get some sleep, I sat and stared at Dame Winifred's gothic manse, looming like the progenitor of evil, replete with spires and gargoyles. Mesmerizing my weary eyes in the stygian predawn. Then a light went on, not in my blurry brain but in a window up behind a spire and two gargoyles. In the wing where Randy Randall had stopped me from searching for Al Jones. I meant to ask him earlier: What's behind that padlocked door? when he was out in the parking lot seeing what all the commotion was about. Before Gleason and Kowalski accosted me.

Randall had been shocked by the second murder but soon became indignant. "Our members will leave in droves," he complained, threatening to have my badge if I fail to "solve these unfortunate incidents immediately and preserve Broken Oak's impeccable reputation." What's he been smoking? Calling cold-blooded murder an unfortunate incident is like calling 9/11 an airplane accident. Randall's obviously the type who talks back to traffic cops and always gets the ticket. Even Gleason and Kowalski, who seem more concerned these days about public reaction to crime than about the cop on the beat, were annoyed at Randall for attacking me. They were more annoyed, however, at his failure to provide coffee and sandwiches. Come to think of it, that also annoyed me.

I climbed out of my car and headed for the light in the window.

CHAPTER TWENTY-THREE

In the massive door frame, the tiny button looked more like a knot than a doorbell. No one answered when I pressed, but I pressed only once, and not too hard. It was 4:00 A.M. and Randy Randall was sawing logs. He's not a bad person, unless he murdered O'Reilly for threatening to form a cartel, buy Broken Oak, raze his beloved aunt's mansion, plow under the golf course, cover it with condos and tract housing. Or put his golf pro up to the deed, then killed him to cover it up.

Who could hear a bell in a mansion this big, anyway? By the time you got to the door, the caller would be gone. Which could be good, if it was a salesperson, a serial killer, or a politician. I considered using the huge wrought iron door knocker that would surely awaken the dead. Instead, I tested the latch, only for Randall's protection of course, and found the door unlocked. He should be more careful with a killer on the loose. Unless it's him. Unless he left the door unlocked for us cops to come in and use the bathroom. Yeah. Right. Randall was so inhospitable we joked about "pulling O'Reilly's" and peeing into the water hazards.

Randall could have left the door unlocked hoping to be robbed and vandalized, giving him an excuse to close the club and collect insurance, while commotion over the murders subsides. He could also be luring me in to bring me up on trespass charges. Maybe he wants my tin badge, like a trophy in the men's grill. Like a tin cup in that Kevin Costner golf movie. Or he could be hiding behind his arras, waiting to whack me with some medieval weapon, a mace or a mashie, with the plausible excuse that he thought I was the killer. Taking a wicked divot in my half-Polack cranium, smiling all the while. Okay. Maybe I *am* letting my imagination run away with me.

I opened the great front door, barely wide enough to slip inside, and quietly shut it behind me. It made no noise at all, which seemed odd for such a heavy door. Only bank vault doors are just as quiet.

It was also uncannily quiet inside the main entrance hall. Dame Winifred, in oil, was still dramatically displayed in a shaft of moonlight through a lead-mullioned window, looking saucier than Escoffier, my wife would have punned. Anyway, moonlight became the grande dame of the mystery genre. The dame must have gotten a kick out of me creeping past her portrait into abyssal darkness, hackles raised like Freddie Kruger's stalking me. Her enigmatic smile, like the Mona Lisa, mocked my consternation at the paltry plot twist of the murder of my prime suspect. It pales compared to her contrivances.

I wished I could bull my way through this place like the day before, when I believed I was in hot pursuit of the horny golf pro. At least hot pursuit has a definite objective, like hitting a golf ball. Golf balls and killers on the lam are often unpredictable, though. At least I remembered how to get upstairs this way. Along the main entrance hall, through a hidden door in the wood paneling, to a stairwell. I only hoped I could find the hidden door in the dark.

Moving like a cat burglar, I finally found the secret latch Randy Randall had showed me. I turned it and the door sighed open, as if I'd loosed Dame Winifred's lacy bodice.

I stepped inside the stairwell, worried about each creaking step betraying my presence. I also worried about Randall waiting at the top of the stairs with a five iron or a fire ax. I had noticed a few fire axes the day before. They are requirements for public buildings, and also Lizzie Borden types.

I could feel the mansion breathing as it exhaled the sigh released by the hidden door. But the breathing suddenly stopped. My progress up the spiral stairs became purely mechanical. Utilitarian, no longer beguiling. The mansion was now annoyed at my intrusion. The formerly randy Dame Winifred had rapidly relaced her bodice and longed to put my neck in a noose.

I pulled my snub-nose from its holster and plodded on.

There were no fiends with five irons or fire axes at the top of the stairs. There was only a long, empty hallway, ending at the door that Randall had refused to open the day before, when I was chasing Al Jones, who was already dead. Unlike yesterday, however, the padlocks were missing, the burglar bars were off, and the door was ajar.

I heard a voice beyond the door and saw the same light I had seen from the parking lot. I opened the door a little wider, slipped inside, and started climbing a short flight of stairs. The voice belonged to Randy Randall. He seemed to be talking to himself. I kept climbing. Though the stairs did not creak in the least, he saw me before I reached the top step.

"Not again," he said, seemingly used to my snub-nose. He *should* be shaking in his boots, after I nearly shot him in the pro shop.

"What are you doing?" I said.

"You first. You're the one who's trespassing."

"I saw the light from outside."

"So what? It's my house and I live here."

"I got worried."

"What about?"

"I thought you might need help. A killer's on the loose, and you could be the next victim."

"How did you get in?"

"The front door was unlocked. You also told me there was nothing—"

I stopped in midsentence. Someone was lying on a cot in the shadows behind Randall.

"Who are you?" I said, shoving my snub-nose at him.

"He's my cousin, Gregory," said Randall.

"He's also a murder suspect."

"I can assure you that he is harmless."

"They all say that. Why didn't you tell me about him before?"

I stepped around Randall and stared at the man on the cot. He was morbidly obese, close to four hundred pounds I'd say, and grinning like an idiot. He looked harmless, seeming unable to swing a golf club or even get up.

"What're you doing here?" I asked him.

"Our aunt's will granted him lodging here for life," Randall answered. "Another reason I need to keep this place going. She left most of her fortune, unfortunately, to the nephew who wants nothing to do with Broken Oak."

"Let Greg talk," I said.

"Gregory can't talk," said Randall.

So it's Gregory.

"A congenital birth defect, Detective. He was born with no larynx."

"Can't they fix it?"

Randall shook his head, as if I should know better.

"Can he move?"

"Enough." Randall frowned, as if I'd asked more than enough questions.

"What does that mean?"

"He can get around, but he has everything he needs right here."

Looking around, I noticed a kitchenette, a small bathroom, a TV, a large bookcase loaded with Dame Winifred's mysteries. I thought of asking if Greg, er, Gregory could read, but, recalling the padlocks on the door, I had a more pertinent question.

"Why do you lock him in?"

"I have a court order," Randall said, as if he had issued it himself. "He needs to be confined."

He also needs a bath, I thought. The room smelled like an old gymnasium.

"Then he *is* dangerous," I said, ready to read Randy the riot act for shielding a suspect and withholding evidence.

"Only to himself," said Randall, like a know-it-all talk radio psychologist tolerating a stupid caller.

"Then why lock him up?" I said, seldom afraid of asking stupid questions.

Continuing to frown, Randall told me, "There is also no reason for him to come in contact with our club members."

"What did he do?" I asked.

"There was an incident, several years ago, where his kindness to a young boy was, shall I say, misinterpreted."

"He's a child molester?"

Randall's eyes narrowed and he snapped, "You cops are all the same! You see only black or white, only right or wrong. There are no gray areas."

"You're dead wrong," I told him, smiling slightly. "I know that laws are subject to interpretation. That's what makes them great, though not so good at times."

"How progressive of you," Randall said, through clenched teeth. "If only you meant it."

"Any way you slice it," I said, "you're obstructing justice."

"With a poor unfortunate," said Randall, suddenly pleading his cousin's case, "who can barely get up and move around?"

"Can he swing a golf club?"

"He can barely put his hands together."

Okay. He's not exactly svelte, but neither was Craig Stadler, aka The Walrus, who managed to win the Masters.

"Did he know about O'Reilly trying to buy this place?"

"He never saw him or Al Jones," Randall insisted.

The cousin continued grinning like the idiot he was. Could he swing a club? He weighed more than two Craig Stadlers, plus Michael Skakel.

"You sure?"

"I can assure you that he has not come out of this room in years."

"Is he left-handed?"

"I have no idea."

"Which hand does he eat with?"

"Both."

I decided not to give the obvious reply but merely asked, "Mind if I look around?"

Randall hesitated, but he knew he was shielding a suspect and had better cooperate.

"Go ahead," he said, grudgingly.

I looked around and found a closet containing pants tailored by Omar the Tentmaker and shoes the size of rowboats. Cousin Gregory couldn't have gotten his big toe into the golf shoes with the missing spike from Al Jones's locker. I found no five iron or any other lethal weapons. The only dresser contained a few pairs of oversized socks, several undershirts, boxer shorts, and scads of prescription bottles.

"What are these for?" I asked. Without my reading glasses, which were in my car along with *Murder on the Moor*, I could not read the labels.

"Nitroglycerin."

"Bad ticker?"

"Any exertion could kill him. I told you he was harmless."

"And he never leaves this room?"

"You're catching on."

And you're an arrogant prick, Mr. Randall. But you could be off the hook, for the moment.

"What's this?" I noticed a shopping bag that was shoved underneath the cot.

"Your guess is as good as mine," Randall shrugged.

I pulled out the bag and picked it up. It was heavy, but the weight instantly disappeared, leaving me holding only the bag by the handles. The bottom had split and hundreds of golf balls bounced crazily across the attic floor.

"Good Lord," said Randall, looking genuinely surprised.

Gregory rolled with laughter, nearly collapsing the cot.

CHAPTER TWENTY-FOUR

It was dawn when I left the clubhouse. Desperate for sleep, decrying man's inhumanity to man. Why can't we all just get along? And then I ran into Dr. Fitch on a cart path between the first tee and practice putting green.

"Good morning," he said, smiling broadly.

"What's so good about it?" I mumbled. He was wearing a puce polo shirt, tangerine Bermudas, canary yellow socks. His varicose veins looked like a road map of Long Island. There's the road to Ronkonkoma.

"Cheer up, Detective," he said. "It's a great golf day."

"God's in His heaven," I told him, "all's right with the world, and the course is still closed."

"But I have an early tee-off time."

He tried walking past me. I stepped in front of him, like a traffic cop, and said, "Al Jones has been murdered."

"That *is* a shame," Fitch said, "but he was not part of my foursome. Is he dead?"

"What part of murder don't you understand?"

"Then you understand that I cannot bring him back."

"I understand that you doctors are used to death, but I would expect anyone to show more emotion." I studied his eyes, which saw right through me.

"I hardly knew him," he said.

"He was your golf pro."

"Not mine, Detective. I took only one lesson from him and he could not help me. He was not a good swing doctor, as they say."

"That's all that matters to you?" I was practically stuttering.

"That and playing on this perfect morning. Please move aside."

"No way. We believe the Jones murder also occurred somewhere out on the course. It's closed indefinitely."

"Are you sure it was murder?" Fitch glared at me. "I could have your badge if he died of natural causes."

"Get in line."

And get in my lineup of suspects. You could have murdered O'Reilly, then Jones found out and threatened to turn you in or tried to blackmail you. But I'll question you later, when I'm good and ready. Now I'm bone tired and borderline irrational. I can't risk flying off the handle. At least I'm pleased to see the patrol cars I ordered coming to close the joint. Fitch noticed them too and started to leave.

"Don't leave town," I told him. "I'll need to question you."

"Catch me if you can," he said. "I am a busy man, with friends in high places." He gave me a cheery wave of dismissal.

I directed a uniform to escort him to his car, mostly to annoy him. I got friends in low places, with blue uniforms.

CHAPTER TWENTY-FIVE

I felt like a fool for watching Al Jones's car while he was dead in the trunk and for not searching the mansion earlier and finding Randy Randall's cousin. Bet I'm a big joke down at headquarters. Bet they're saying I can't find my nose in front of my face, and it's time to take a desk job or retire. I'll show 'em. But what to do next?

Back home in Bayville, I was so tired I couldn't sleep. I have trouble sleeping during the day anyway. Carol was great at it. She could curl up anywhere and take catnaps. I loved to watch her sleep. She looked so contented. Until she got sick and her naps grew longer and longer. Eventually deep, uncontrollable sleeps. Day and night, until the big sleep.

I lay on my bed and wrapped a pillow around my head, but the sun kept finding my tired eyes. Light has too much pressure. All those waves and particles coming at you so fast, like so many murder suspects.

The young couple upstairs was also keeping me awake by moaning louder than usual. Bedsprings squeaking to beat the band. Why don't they get up and go to work? How can they make the rent money while making the beast with two backs every hour of the day? That was an expression my wife preferred to "humping like camels." She told me Shakespeare said it.

I retrieved *Murder on the Moor* from my bedroom trash can, where I had tossed it when I first got home, displeased with Detective Peter H. Couloir's antiquated methods and frustrated by my own fuckups. At least the little tome could put me to sleep and I needed that. Perhaps it had put Carol into that final coma.

I collated the loose pages and finally found my place. Couloir had just discovered Algernon Spotswood's body in the steamer trunk on the Orient Express. Algie must have been pretty ripe. But Couloir seemed not to notice, another detail, or lack thereof, which annoyed me. Maybe it's mentioned in the few pages beyond that are missing. Now Couloir's back at the earl of Cranbrook's estate, where the brash American, Marty Phelps, was murdered on the moor. Couloir is confronting the earl in his study.

"We know that Monsieur Spotswood was murdered with a Webley-Vickers .44 caliber pistol. Precisely the type of weapon that was used in the first murder. Perhaps the very same weapon that is missing from your collection."

Too bad there was no ballistics back then. Couloir could easily match the bullets and nail whoever has the gun. If he can find it. It must be this earl character. At least it was easier to find a particular gun in the old days, before everyone and their brother were packing.

"Would you like some brandy?" asked the Earl, ringing for a servant. "You've had a long trip, to the continent and back. And in so short a time. Truly an Herculean effort, my dear fellow. You must be exhausted."

You cunning SOB. Trying to throw the little tec off the scent by blowing smoke up his butt and getting him loaded. I'm sure he can see right through you.

"*I must decline, monsieur,*" said Couloir. "*I napped often during the trip, and I am quite rested. In fact, I have all my faculties.*"

Good case for napping, and a good slap at the arrogant earl. Also a warning that he's hot on the killer's trail.

"*I would ask one favor,*" Couloir continued, "*if you would be so kind.*"

The Earl said, "*Name it.*"

"*I would like to search the premises.*"

"*That may be arranged. But why? There was no foul play in here. Of that I can assure you. The first unfortunate incident occurred well out on the moor. And Algie was surely shot on the Orient Express.*"

Watch it, Couloir. This earl's full of crap.

"*I have reason to believe that Monsieur Spotswood was shot right here, in this very house. And it was here that his body was placed into one of your own steamer trunks, then shipped to La Gare du Nord, where it was placed on the train.*"

"*By whom?*"

"*Porters, of course, merely doing their duty.*"

"*One of my steamer trunks, you say?*"

"*Précisement.*"

"*Preposterous!*"

"*We shall see. Now, if you please, I shall get on with my search.*"

"*And you expect to find the murder weapon?*"

"*Your Webley-Vickers? Perhaps.*"

Another slap at the earl. I liked it. Couloir is stubbornly searching the earl's mansion. He's coming up empty, however, like my initial search for Al Jones. A few more pages are missing, but they don't seem to matter. The story continued with Couloir and the earl proceeding down a long, dark hallway filled with sinister-looking family portraits and an arras, as Randy Randall calls those big curtains, ending at a locked door leading to what the earl claims is an abandoned wing.

"Please open it," Couloir said.

"Surely, there is no need," the Earl said indignantly.

"With all due respect, I must insist."

"I do not believe I have the key."

Don't believe him, Couloir. Randy Randall tried the same stall on me. I should have made him open the door to his cousin's room, or busted it down. If I had discovered the fat cousin sooner, I could have found Jones's body sooner and avoided looking like a fool. Don't make my stupid mistakes.

"I am in no hurry, monsieur. I shall wait right here, until the key is located."

Good-bye, Earl.

Grudgingly, the Earl patted his jacket pockets, produced a small key . . .

I knew that the earl, and Randy Randall, had the key all along.

. . . and unlocked the door . . .

Now I'll never get to sleep.

. . . then he slowly pushed it open, saying, "Wait here a moment, while I find the light switch."

He slipped through the doorway, and was lost a moment in the blackness within. Suddenly, there was the sound of a struggle, a flash of light, and the deafening roar of a gunshot. The lights in the room came on, and the Earl, a smoking Webley-Vickers .44 in his hand, was standing over a man's body.

"My word," said the Earl. "It's Uncle Esmond! Is he dead?"

"Certainement, monsieur. The wound is massive, and directly through the center of his chest."

"He tried to strike me with this." The Earl examined the Webley-Vickers.

"Would it be the weapon that has been missing from your collection?"

"I-I am afraid it is."

"If you don't mind, monsieur, I will feel safer if you give it to me."

Is he nuts? The earl just drilled a hole the size of the Brooklyn Battery Tunnel through his weird uncle Esmond, he's holding the smoking gun, and Couloir's politely asking for it? Grab it, you wimp, and slap the arrogant earl silly.

The Earl handed over the gun, but added indignantly, "I must inform you that I am quite capable of handling all sorts of firearms. Especially this particular Webley. As I have already told you, my good man, it served me quite well in the Crimea."

"And it discharged by accident in the struggle?"

Now he's got him. The gun didn't go off by accident. The earl's obviously lying through his aristocratic teeth.

"I nearly had control," said the Earl, "but he was fighting me. Uncle Esmond took the Webley from my collection, used it twice for his dastardly deeds, and was about to use it on me."

"His motive?"

"Jealousy, one would suspect. He and Martin Phelps were rivals for the affection of a certain lady, as I have already told you."

"So you . . ."

So you asked him again to see if he sticks with his story. I do that all the time. I also theorized that Phelps was fooling around, as his wife was doing with Spotswood.

". . . but what about Monsieur Spotswood?"

The Earl shrugged as though the second murder also did not matter, and said, "Perhaps old Algie saw my uncle removing the Webley from my display case, or trying to get rid of it in some manner. And as for shipping him out on the Orient Express, that's a dead giveaway, if you'll pardon the pun. Uncle Esmond had that sort of imagination."

"Hmm, an interesting theory."

Don't believe it. More than a few modern-day homicide detectives I know would swallow it hook, line, and sinker, not because they lack little gray cells but because they worry about pressure from politicos, the brass, the media, and adding to their murders-solved column. There's also too many pages left in the book to support the earl's theory.

The young couple upstairs was still making the bedsprings squeak. The sun was slanting directly through my blinds and into my face. The plot was thickening, with Peter H. Couloir hot on the trail of the arrogant earl. I nodded off anyway, letting the little paperback hit my bedroom floor.

CHAPTER TWENTY-SIX

Running a murder investigation is like running a marathon. You gotta go the distance and you can't stop for long. I slept about an hour, hopped out of bed, downed a cup of instant coffee, and drove to Al Jones's condo.

He rented a place at the Hamlet, an agglomeration of trendy apartments with an Anglophile name designed to attract yuppies and lothario golf pros. Long Island has more Hamlets than Olivier ever performed. No wonder Dame Winifred settled here.

Without the uniformed cop posted outside, Jones's condo would have been difficult to find. It shared too many sharp roofs, slanted windows, snug balconies with all the others. Residents could easily reach out and mistakenly, or unmistakenly, grab a neighbor's martini or main squeeze. Part of design these days? I only know there are too many angles in this architecture for uncomplicated cops. Like too many plot twists in *Murder on the Moor* and too many suspects at Broken Oak.

I parked close to Jones's condo, hopped out of my car, and walked briskly toward the uniform, a rookie I recognized. I pretended I had a good night's sleep and was ten years younger.

"Any breaks yet?" the rookie asked.

"You get all the breaks with gigs like this," I told him.

"Yeah," he said. "I love guarding evidence."

"We've all paid our dues," I reminded. "But what do you college kids know?"

"Only that we know nothing."

"That's a good lesson. Forensics been here yet?"

The rookie shook his head.

I slowly opened the front door, wary of smearing any fingerprints, and stepped carefully inside. It's always creepy examining the effects of murder victims. I get the feeling they're watching, upset that a stranger's poking through their private stuff. I'm only trying to bring their killer to justice. Somewhere along the line, precious articles, carefully collected and jealously hoarded, lose all their sentimentality. Treasures become junk. I would never be able to throw out Carol's clothing and junk. While they filled her closets and dresser drawers, it seemed she was coming back home.

The condo was too damn tidy. A bachelor boy from Texas should have left his bed unmade and most of his dirty clothes lying around, along with a few empty Lone Star long-necks. But this place was neater than a pin or a putting green. It bothered me. There was also no golf paraphernalia. Not a single club, bag, tee, ball. I would not find the five iron that whacked O'Reilly, or much else.

Jones's choice of reading material, or lack thereof, also bothered me. I had not expected to find the complete works of Aleksandr I. Solzhenitsyn or Dame Winifred's mysteries, but I thought I might find a copy of *Golf Digest*, *Stock Car Racing*, *World Wrestling*, *Baseball*, *The Ring*, *Hustler*. You can learn a lot from the victim's reading material. But I was learning nothing. There was only a crisp new issue of the *New Yorker*, which I suspected did not belong to Jones, lying conspicuously alone on a coffee table.

All of Jones's clothing was clean and carefully folded. Either he was a neat-freak or someone had tidied up. Was there a maid? I made a mental note to check. Or a girlfriend? There seemed to be a woman's touch here. Mrs. O'Reilly's?

Apart from clothing, the lack of personal effects was distressing. No jewelry, loose change, lucky pieces, golf trophies, memorabilia from his baseball days, card decks, condoms. The condo felt like a fresh motel room, minus Gideon's Bible. A nonsmoking room. No cigarette butts, traces of snuff, partial plugs of chewing tobacco.

In years of poring over personal effects of the suddenly deceased, I always found the remnants of at least one bad habit. Except for boffing O'Reilly's wife, Jones appeared to be a Boy Scout. Even the kitchen was clean as a whistle. Only milk, butter, and eggs were in the fridge. What manner of man would not be chilling a six-pack? I could have used a cold brew for breakfast. Even at the risk of smearing a few prints and disillusioning the rookie.

Forensics should be here by now. They probably stopped for coffee. Cops do too much waiting because, contrary to popular movie and TV images, there are no convenient time warps and jump cuts.

I soon grew impatient. I had places to go and people to see. I sat on the living room couch, where I was least likely to disturb anything. At least I had not brought *Murder on the Moor* with me. I risked flipping through the *New Yorker*, however, past brummagem blow-ins begging subscriptions and mail orders for bubble bath and bomber jackets.

Something other than tawdry ads and blow-ins was also among the pages. I slipped it out with the point of my penknife. A newspaper clipping with a group photograph and caption. Al Jones was displaying his trophy for winning the Long Island Open, held at Broken Oak. He was also shaking hands with the tournament chairman, none other than Dr. Fitch. The Gothic mansion and its turrets loomed in the background. Randy Randall looked on like Gomez Addams. Mr. and Mrs. O'Reilly were also in the group, along with Vince Henry, the black greenskeeper. Slim, Jones's caddy, stood off to the side, grinning and displaying his rotten teeth.

CHAPTER TWENTY-SEVEN

"The same club that killed O'Reilly killed Al Jones," the ME informed me, across from Jones's body on the autopsy table.

"A five iron?"

"The head wounds are identical, as is the ash residue."

"Really?" I was surprised at the normally circumspect ME offering an opinion so early in the autopsy.

"I'm not into the chest cavity yet," the ME grinned, "but I plucked his brain like a grape."

He shoved a rubber-gloved fist into the empty cranium, twisted it around, and pulled it out with a loud popping sound he made with his tongue.

"I get the idea," I said. "But I won't puke or pass out. You sure it's the same five iron?"

"I'd stake my reputation on it."

"What makes you so certain?"

"Shape of the wound, blade angle of 30 degrees, edges and grooves like gun barrels have rifling."

"You can match the blade of a club to dead flesh, like bullets to a gun barrel?"

"And we can match these ashes, without even using a microscope. Look for yourself, Detective."

I moved to the ME's side of the autopsy table and stared at the awful gash near the occipital bone.

"See 'em?" the ME said, shoving me closer.

"It's better if I stay back," I said. "I don't have my reading glasses," though it was the smell, not lack of magnification, that made me back off.

"Of course we'll test the ashes and make certain," he said.

"Then we'll know it's the same club?"

"When you find it."

"But you said—"

"The blade angle and measurement of the wounds on our two victims are similar, but flesh doesn't take a perfect imprint. Remember Julius Caesar?"

"I'm more familiar with Julius Boros, who won the U.S. Open before you were born."

"Remember that even if someone's stabbed repeatedly, like Caesar, and the wounds *appear* identical, still we can never be sure it's the same knife."

"Then what good is forensics?"

"Find the five iron. If the ashes are still on it, we'll know it was used in both murders."

"Even if I do find it, and there's got to be thousands of them out there, I won't know who used it."

"It may have some prints," the ME said, the eternal optimist. I couldn't blame him. When you're performing autopsies all day, you need to look at the bright side once in a while.

"And I could hit the Lotto," I said, with a half smile.

"At least we know it was swung by a lefty," he told me. "Unlike the first murder, however, this fellow was facing his killer. And Jones wasn't killed near his car. When your heart stops, you stop bleeding, and we didn't find enough blood in the trunk or anywhere else."

"The body had to be lifted into the trunk," I said, "which couldn't have been easy. Particularly for the average woman, unless she had some help."

"Got a female suspect, preferably a weight lifter?"

"I've got one can get it up," I said, picturing Mrs. O bouncing naked out at the end of her diving board.

"Hook her up to a lie detector."

"First let me get this straight. The same club that killed O'Reilly could have killed Jones."

"Correct."

"But it can't be proved beyond a reasonable doubt."

"If you can't find the club or it has no ashes."

"And the club was right-handed but swung by a lefty."

"Correct again."

"But Jones was facing the killer," I said, "and O'Reilly's back was turned."

"That's the long and the short of it," the ME said. "So is this . . ."

He pulled back the sheet covering Jones's lower abdomen, exposing his manhood.

"That *is* a Texas longhorn," I said.

"And O'Reilly was hung like a stud gerbil," said the ME. "Hey. Aren't you—"

"Don't you have anything else to do but size up the stiffs?" I said. No pun intended.

"Do you know that dead men can have erections, Detective? And that we can tell before we undress them?"

"I give up. How can you tell?"

"They die with a smile on their face. And one more thing," the ME continued. "It's about your golf shoes, with the heel spike missing."

"They're not mine," I said.

"They're not this guy's either. Look at his feet."

I looked. They were too big for the shoes. Maybe there is some connection between big feet and a big schlong.

CHAPTER TWENTY-EIGHT

I stopped at a neighborhood bar called Sand City on my way
home that evening. It's only half a mile from my house on
Bayville Avenue. I should have gone straight home, but I
needed a drink and wanted to avoid drinking alone.

The bartender and I made small talk, though I had bigger
fish to fry and was in the frying pan with them. I ordered
only beer. Avoiding shots, liquid and leaden, I watched the
sun sinking beyond Connecticut across the Sound. I let the
long, unproductive day slip behind me, imagining happier
days as lights in Greenwich gradually flickered on. As husbands and wives chatted on porches and patios, with chil-
dren flocking back to their nests when it grew too dark to
ride a bike or see a ball. I wished that Carol and I were still
quietly conversing on our patio without a care in the world.
I also wished I had watched more sunsets with her instead
of hanging around the nineteenth hole.

Though she had no interest in golf, Carol was great at
discussing murder cases with me, sifting the clues instead of
flailing at them, calming me down and pointing me in the

right direction. Showing me the way. The way Dame Winifred's little fictional dick would do it? Couloir means passageway in French, she once told me, ever the teacher. She also told me that neatness counts, whether coloring with fat crayons or collecting bullets and blood samples. I told her that's easy to say when all your violence and gore happen on the printed page. Or offstage, like *Murder on the Moor*. I should have given her more credit. She would have asked right away if the golf shoes with the missing heel spike fit Al Jones's feet. She would also have had some inclination as to who had planted them in his locker. That's your killer, *sans doute*, she would have told me, as assuredly as Peter H. Couloir. I kicked myself for scoffing at some of her conclusions and accusing her of reading too many murder mysteries and then ordered another beer.

Now I'm reduced to traipsing around and finding out whose feet fit those damn shoes, like Prince Charming's pathetic old envoy desperately seeking Cinderella with the glass slipper. As if it will do any good. At least I know they're too small for Randy Randall's obese cousin and too large for Mrs. O'Reilly, who's suddenly entering Sand City.

What's she doing here? I'm not ready for her yet. I've got a good buzz going, and I planned to question her tomorrow. I prefer catching my suspects by surprise. So they stammer, stall, and screw up their alibis. Now I'm more likely to stammer and stall, thanks to the short shorts and see-through T-shirt she's barely wearing. I should hide behind the bar with my rumpled jacket and stained necktie, but she's already seen me.

"Detective Kanopka?" she said brightly, though her deep blue eyes looked slightly tired. "What a pleasant surprise."

"Come here often?" I asked, hoping it didn't sound like a pickup line.

The bartender overheard us and smiled.

"You haven't answered my question," I said, studying her facial expression, distracted by several wisps of her soft blond hair falling out of place.

"Never with any tall Texas golf pros," Mrs. O told me, reading my mind, brushing back the hairs as if they were Brillo and not spun gold. Mounting the bar stool beside me like a lap dancer, causing her short shorts to rise even higher, exposing even more of her long, lithe legs.

I did not believe her. Bayville's little bars and remoteness were perfect for cheaters. She and Al Jones could have been cuddling in one of Sand City's corner booths, even when I was here. If she had worn those shorts, however, I would have noticed her.

"Gin and tonic?" she asked the bartender, who did not seem to recognize her.

"It's on me," I said.

"Thank you, Detective."

She held her glass in her right hand, but she could be a lefty. Could she swing a golf club well enough to fell a guy Jones's size, then dump the body into his trunk? What would her reaction be to news of the murder? I was about to tell her about it and find out, until the TV above the bar did it for me.

"There's been another brutal murder on Long Island," a local anchorman began, "at the exclusive Broken Oak Country Club."

I stared at Mrs. O as she stared at the TV screen, eyes widening, jaw dropping, full lips looking even more inviting. Get ahold of yourself, Kanopka, and stop drinking.

"The bludgeoned body of golf pro Al Jones was found in the trunk of his car," the anchorman continued as the camera panned the links, the Crown Vic, the mansion. The bulletin ended with an on-site reporter linking it to O'Reilly's murder and suggesting a serial killer.

As regular programming resumed, Mrs. O, with an expression close to disgust, said, "Why didn't you tell me?"

"I didn't think you cared," I said offhandedly.

"You were watching my reaction," she snapped.

"It's my job." Wake up, Kanopka. She's not all sweetness and light.

"And I suppose the taxpayers, which also means me, are paying for my gin and tonic?"

That bothered me. The drink was out-of-pocket.

"I wasn't—"

"Buying for a black widow?"

"I didn't—"

"And I did not murder my golf pro or my husband."

I almost believed her. But I've met many cold-blooded killers who can beat both the lie detector and the good old wham-bam. They're also crazy, which can give them the strength of Olympic weight lifters.

"Your husband was sleeping around, you know."

"That's part of why we were getting divorced. Remember?"

"And Al Jones was sleeping with the members' wives. And maybe he dumped you, so you killed him."

She smiled and sipped her gin and tonic, suddenly not mad at me.

"If you must know," she said, "Al Jones tried coming on to me more than once during my lessons. He said that my shoulder muscles tighten too much and my arms get too close together. He was always telling me not to squeeze the goodies. I don't like men who think they can get away with anything."

"I feel the same way about certain women," I said, imagining her *goodies* bursting through that thin cotton T-shirt.

"Al Jones did not get away with anything with me," Mrs. O insisted. "He was tall and handsome, but it takes more than looks to win me over."

I like hearing that from certain women.

"You come here often?" I'm not giving up.

"Not really."

"What are the odds?"

"Of what?"

"Of all the gin joints in the world . . ." I imitated Bogie in *Casablanca*, badly.

She laughed and confessed, "I only come here to eat. I've always had a good appetite, even under the direst circumstances. If I'm ever on death row, I'll order one hell of a last meal."

"Or one last roll in the hay with a horse-hung stud like Al Jones?"

"Maybe I *should* have gotten to know him a little better."

"You knew him pretty well in this photo." I showed her the newspaper clipping from Jones's condo.

She studied it and said, "That's when he won the tournament last year. My husband was a big golf fan. Jones's win was a big deal at the time. I was told that local pros don't win too many tournaments. And my husband said I might learn something."

What else did he have in mind? Setting her up with the stud golf pro, catching them in the act, swinging the divorce proceedings in his favor?

"I might learn something," I said, "by searching your house again. This time, more thoroughly."

"Be my guest. I've been evicted."

Her eyes narrowed and her shoulders tensed, as if she believed that I had something to do with it. But her husband's creditors, coming out of the woodwork, had the estate held in escrow.

"I'm staying at the Tides Motel, just down the street," she added, relaxing somewhat, sipping her drink.

"It's tidy," I shrugged.

She laughed, like Carol, who also liked puns.

We ordered burgers and ate at the bar. I switched from beer to seltzer and lime. I was perfectly sober when we were finished eating and she asked, "Would you like to come back to the Tides with me?"

CHAPTER TWENTY-NINE

My tenants were away that evening. Though I normally enjoyed their presence upstairs, I did not need to hear them humping to beat the band, reminding me of what I could be doing at the Tides with Mrs. O'Reilly. If I slept with my suspects or anyone other than my wife, that is.

I fell into bed with randy Dame Winifred instead. *Murder on the Moor*'s binding split further and a few more loose pages fell out. Unlike loose women, however, I respected the tattered little tome more and more with each acquaintance. I reinserted the pages and started reading.

The evil earl of Cranbrook had just shot his weird uncle Esmond as they struggled for the Webley-Vickers .44 that was stolen from the earl's gun collection. The same gun had also killed Algernon Spotswood, a sportsman friend of the earl's who was stuffed into a steamer trunk on the Orient Express, and Marty Phelps, the American found murdered out on the earl's moor. The arrogant earl had accused Uncle Esmond of murdering Phelps over the affections of the mysterious Lady Barkworth and murdering Spotswood for seeing him with the gun, perhaps trying to replace it in the earl's collection.

I like a mystery with a few good twists, but I don't like being tied up in knots. I was also impatient for Peter H. Couloir, currently questioning Lady Barkworth, to straighten things out.

Lady Barkworth herself answered the door . . .

Ain't life tough when the servants are off? I skipped the nuances of dealing with the nobility and went to the real dialogue. Where Couloir, if he has any balls, will ask the tough questions.

"Yes, Detective, I did know Martin Phelps. His demise was indeed tragic and untimely. But why ever have you come to me about it?"

"Your Ladyship is very, may I say, close with the Earl of Cranbrook and his family. Are you not?"

"What are you driving at, Detective?"

"The Earl's uncle has been shot and killed."

"Esmond? No!"

"I am sorry. I know that you and he were—"

"What?"

"Please excuse me. It is only with your most kind indulgence that I am merely trying to establish, only for my own records, of course, a complete background for this murder case."

"You are trying, Detective. Indeed, quite trying. And I am quite busy. I must bid you good day."

Don't let her throw you, Couloir. This so-called lady's bark is worse than her bite.

"I must ask one further question. It has been suggested that Esmond, Martin Phelps, and Your Ladyship were, shall I say, involved. And that the first murder resulted from a quarrel over Your Ladyship's affections."

"Who on earth told you that?"

"We have our sources and, with all due respect, they must remain confidential."

"Have your sources also told you that I was involved with Algernon Spotswood?"

"Why, no."

"And that I had assassinated Archduke Francis Ferdinand and set off the Great War?"

She's feisty, like Mrs. O. She must also be a knockout, though Dame Winifred supplies no physical description or mention of her age. Real cops need details, though a woman's age usually remains a mystery.

"I must remind Your Ladyship that this is a murder investigation, and not a matter for levity."

"Nor for preposterous, insolent accusations, Detective. Now, I must bid you good day."

She turned, imperiously, and glided away, leaving Couloir to mutter, almost inaudibly, "Thank you for your cooperation, Your Ladyship."

Crap. The chapter's ended. Lady Barkworth could have plugged Marty Phelps, maybe even Algie. Or someone could have put her up to it. Like the evil earl himself? His weird uncle Esmond? There's also the gamekeeper to contend with. So many suspects you need a scorecard. There was a scorecard of sorts: a page at the front of the book listing the cast of characters. But it fell out long ago and I lost it.

CHAPTER THIRTY

"Recognize these?" I asked, setting the golf shoes with the missing spike on Randy Randall's desk.

"They're the shoes you found in Al Jones's locker," Randall said, shrugging and turning up his palms, as if saying So what? His know-it-all attitude irritated me, plus the fact that he looked none the worse from staying up so late the other night. His posture was square, his eyes were bright and every hair on his head was perfectly in place. I felt disheveled and dog-tired. "Please don't let those shoes scratch my Chippendale desk," he added.

"They're a perfect match for the heel print we found at the water hazard," I told him, "next to O'Reilly's body. We believe the killer was wearing them."

"Then Al Jones is your killer."

"These shoes don't fit him. Not even close."

I watched Randy's face for some sign of surprise, or relief, but his expression remained even.

"How did they get in his locker?" he asked.

"I thought you might be able to help me with that," I said, hoping to rattle him or elicit some emotion. "Mind trying them on?"

"I'm not a golfer," he told me, without even shaking his head or opening his mouth.

"The killer didn't have to be one either." I raised an eyebrow.

"I'm also not a killer." His eyes narrowed and he adjusted his necktie, which didn't need it. Was I finally getting to him?

"Mind trying them on?" I repeated.

"They could have fungus." He winced and shifted uneasily, as if mold spores were worse than murder.

"Believe me," I assured him, "after the way forensics goes through them, they're sterile."

"I don't like trying on someone else's shoes," he said.

"Try 'em on now," I told him, "or try 'em on in court."

Holding one of the shoes at arm's length, like a piece of litter he'd found, Randall slid it onto his foot gingerly. "See?" he said triumphantly. "I'm swimming in it."

"So you are." I took back the shoe and slipped it into its evidence bag with the other.

"Am I absolved, Detective?"

"What about your cousin Gregory?" I wondered if the big lout was still lying on his cot.

"He's at least a 14, quadruple-E, depending on his diet and water retention."

"You understand that I need to confirm that?"

"As you understand that I always cooperate with the law."

Sure. We're both lying through our teeth. I know that cousin Gregory's feet are too big. I only want to show him the shoes to see if there's some spark of recognition. Randall's blowing smoke up my butt.

On our way to Gregory's room, I showed Randall the group photo I had found in Al Jones's condo.

"I remember that tournament," Randall said. "It was last September; we drew crowds of thousands and we were cleaning up for weeks. The course was trampled beyond belief. My greenskeeper nearly quit."

"Don't blame me. I wasn't here." I had wanted to come and watch, but I was working around the clock then and Carol was dying.

"Why is Dr. Fitch in this photo?"

"He was tournament chairman, even though he's not exactly a fan."

"He plays enough."

"Enough golf, but he was no fan of our former pro. He tried more than once to get Jones fired."

"Jones make a play for Fitch's wife?" I was scrambling for answers.

"I don't believe so. It must have been some slight, real or imagined, to himself or a friend." Randall adjusted his necktie again, which still didn't need it. "But Al Jones was a good pro. Despite what you may think, Detective, I am willing to defend some of my help. Even against certain vociferous members."

"Calling Fitch vociferous is putting it mildly," I said.

"He does have a temper. I also defend our members." Randy puffed up like a balloon.

"We also found a pair of panties in a sand trap, not far from O'Reilly's body, that could have belonged to Mrs. Fitch, plus a condom that could have belonged to Jones." Could I burst Randy's balloon?

"You should see what we found after the tournament," he said, merely deflating. I pictured bushel baskets of condoms and panties. "The local youths," he added, "are always sneaking out onto the course late at night, doing the wild thing."

"Was Jones playing more than golf with some other member's wife?" I asked. Let's see what he knows about Mrs. O.

"I'm always the last to know." He went to his necktie again, misaligning it this time.

"Would you have fired him?"

"Of course." Randy reassumed his pompous balloon stance.

"Of course, you'd have a hell of a time finding another pro in the middle of the summer."

"Another good reason, Detective, for me not to murder him."

"Touché," I said, "as your aunt's tec might say."

Randall smiled, slyly.

"I thought you kept this door locked," I said, as we reached Gregory's room.

"Only when the club's open," Randy said. "It's unnecessary for my cousin to meet the members."

"Or to murder them?"

"I've already told you he's harmless."

The obese cousin had been checked out already. Except for molesting a little boy ten years earlier when he attended a school for the handicapped, as Randall earlier admitted, Gregory had no priors.

We entered the room. Gregory was snoring.

"That's loud," I said.

Randall said, "It's normal for someone his size."

"Let's wake him up." I readied the golf shoes.

The cot looked ready to collapse under the excess weight and snores that cannonaded off the rafters.

"Wake up!" I shouted at the supine colossus.

The snoring continued, and I poked Gregory viciously with my fist. It was like kneading a ball of dough. After several tries, I finally gave up and pulled up the sheet to expose his bare feet.

"They're huge," I admitted.

"You couldn't get those shoes on his big toe," Randall said. Did I hear a small sigh of relief?

"Who else can I try?" I asked, rhetorically.

"Our men's locker room attendant," Randall shrugged.

"Where's he been?"

"Out sick."

Just what I need. Another suspect.

CHAPTER THIRTY-ONE

I went alone to the men's locker room to find the attendant. He found me.

"You a member?" he asked, knowing better.

"You take care of the golf shoes?" I flashed my ID.

"And anything else the members need," the attendant said, wearily.

"You been out sick?" I asked.

"Nothin' too serious, but I missed all the action."

"You're lucky."

"How's that?"

"You'd be a suspect." You still are, but I'm trying to get you to let down your guard. A tactic Peter H. Couloir would term *très habilé.*

"You look like you should still be home in bed," I added. He looked like death warmed over, with a pallid complexion and bags under his eyes.

"We can't all be cops," he said, "with great medical benefits."

"Recognize these?" I showed him the golf shoes with the missing spike.

"Polish 'em for you," he said. "No charge."

"They're not mine, and I don't need them polished. The question is, Do you recognize them?"

He examined the shoes and said, "I'll also replace the missing heel spike."

"Thanks, but no thanks. I only need to know if you recognize them. I got them from Al Jones's locker."

"They can't be his. His feet were too big," pronounced the attendant smartly.

"Ever work in forensics?" He had a good eye.

"They do look a little familiar." The attendant turned the brown-and-white saddle shoe over and over, trying to remember. "But there's so many shoes just like these."

"I know. It's a good brand, but they're sold everywhere."

"I know all the members," the attendant continued. "After twenty years of handing out soap and towels in the men's shower room. Get it? The male members? I've seen 'em all."

"Could we stick to their shoes?"

"Well, I polish their street shoes when they go out for a round. When they come back, I polish their golf shoes and clean the spikes. I couldn't have got these."

"Why not?"

"I replace any spikes that are missing."

"Was Mr. O'Reilly a good tipper?"

"That cheapskate? I don't mean any disrespect for the dead," the attendant crossed himself and said, "but Mr. O'Reilly always said he was short when he picked up his shoes. He would promise to take care of me later, but he never did."

"These aren't his shoes?"

"No way. I remember his very well."

"How about Dr. Fitch?"

"Average tipper, always in a hurry. God help me if I didn't have his shoes ready." He crossed himself again.

"What about his temper?" I asked.

"He has more fits than a tailor at Sy Syms," the attendant said. "Get it? Fits, tailor?"

"I'd love to hear more," I said, "but tell me about the hand towels."

"Right over here," the attendant said, leading me to a box of paper towels in a supply closet.

"Can I have some of these?" Forensics had found paper fibers on the golf shoes. Maybe these would match. Georgia-Pacific.

"Take as many as you want," the attendant shrugged.

"Thanks." I handed him a double sawbuck.

Brightening, as if O'Reilly had finally tipped him, the attendant said, "Wait a minute."

"Not another joke?"

"Those golf shoes. I know who owns them. It just hit me."

Along with the double sawbuck? Cynicism is also one of my strong points.

"Who?"

"They belong to Dr. Fitch."

CHAPTER THIRTY-TWO

Slim was slouched in his dilapidated armchair outside the caddy shack, alone. King of the caddies on his throne, holding court over nothing. A smoldering cigarette for a scepter. A bottle of guinea red in a brown paper bag for breakfast.

"Welcome to my humble abode," he said as I approached.

"You told me you weren't living here," I said.

"Just an expression I use on my yacht." At my sour expression, he inquired, "Where's your sense of humor, Detective?"

"Where are the other caddies?"

"Gone to other clubs. Can't make a livin' when the course is closed."

"Why don't *you* go to another club?"

"I like it right here."

Slim grinned, displaying his rotten teeth. That bottle in the brown paper bag must anesthetize them, as well as justify God's ways to man.

"You're living in this shack, aren't you?" I said, wondering how much cheap wine he had imbibed.

"I ain't breakin' no laws," said Slim, waving the bottle. Nothing spilled out. There wasn't much left.

"And our beds are too soft and the food's too good?" I added, letting him know I could lock him up.

"That ain't funny."

"Where's your sense of humor?"

"It disappeared when you closed the course, along with my income."

"Your unreported income?" Accusing a suspect of tax evasion often clears the head even quicker than the good old wham-bam.

"So lock me up." Slim shrugged, well aware that the IRS has much bigger fish to fry.

"You're used to it, aren't you?" I said, hoping to hit where it hurt.

"I done some time," he admitted, "but it was only petty theft. I needed to eat."

"Smoke and drink?"

"We all got vices," Slim said, stubbing his cigarette butt on the exposed chair frame, then tossing it into the traces of a small campfire at his feet.

"What have you been cooking?" I asked.

"Squirrel." Slim grinned and picked at something between his teeth.

"That's disgusting," I said.

"So lock me up."

"They don't serve squirrel in the slam." Thankfully. I know they're rodents and often a nuisance, but they're cute and Carol liked them.

"I'll suffer."

"Who suffered the loss of those sneakers?" I asked, looking at his feet.

"Like 'em?" Slim stretched his long legs.

"Where'd you get them?" I affected my Sam's Club security guard expression. "They look expensive."

"You think I took a five-finger discount?" Slim squirmed slightly.

"Correct me if I'm wrong," I said, "but caddies don't make all that much."

"We walk all day," said Slim. "They're an investment."

"Why don't you wear spikes?"

"We're not allowed. The members' spikes tear up the turf more than enough. Shows you what they know. I can still tear it up, with great golf scores."

Sure. And I'm Tiger Woods. "Recognize these?" I showed him the shoes with the missing spike.

Slim shook his head, took a swig from the brown paper bag, and offered it to me.

"Own any golf shoes?" I asked, declining his offer.

"I've played a time or two," he said. "I got a sweet swing."

"So you've told me." Was he really a good golfer or was the wine talking? "When do you play?"

"Used to play here on Mondays, when the club's closed. Can't no more. They claim the course needs a day of rest, like God created it."

"Who decided?"

"The gods of the greens committee, but I can beat every one of 'em."

"They know you're lighting fires out here?" I did not want to sound like Smokey the Bear, but I needed to keep Slim's feet to the fire.

"I could freeze my friggin' nuts off at night."

"You're not supposed to be here at night."

"Sometimes I hang around a little too late and fall asleep. I got permission." Slim was looking belligerent.

"You got a problem."

"I need a kerosene heater?" he asked. I could smell that dago red on his breath.

"You were here when O'Reilly was murdered. I also know you were here when Al Jones was murdered." I didn't know, but even Peter H. Couloir would have admired my effrontery.

"So what?" Slim sat up straight.

"You'd better tell me all you know." I stepped closer.

"Well . . ."

"Lay it on me." I stepped even closer.

"Okay." He shifted uneasily. "I seen someone out here, real late, night before last."

"The night Al Jones was murdered."

"Can't I get somethin' for telling you this?"

I ignored his shifty plea for coop money. "Who was it?"

"The greenskeeper, Vince Henry."

"What's unusual about that?"

"He's never here at night," Slim explained, suddenly as expansive as the locker room attendant after I tipped him. "He was also in a big friggin' hurry."

"You sure it was him?"

"He ain't that black and it wasn't that dark. He passed right by me in this chair. Thought I was, you know."

"Asleep?"

"Takin' a nap," Slim said indignantly. "I don't live here, don't forget."

Of course you don't. "Was your campfire going?"

"I was freezin' my friggin' nuts."

I can believe that. A golf course can get chilly at night.

"Tell me about Vince Henry," I told him. "Where was he coming from, where was he going?"

"From the parking lot."

"How did you know?"

"I could see his headlights from here."

"You sure they were his?" What were you drinking? How many fingers am I holding up?

"There were no other cars," Slim insisted. "I was in the parking lot a few minutes earlier."

"Stealing hubcaps? You don't have a car."

"Walkin' around, tryin' to keep warm."

"The greenskeeper was running?"

"Toward his shed. In the middle of the night. But don't ask me what time. I ain't got no watch. It's broke. So am I. Can't I get nothin'?"

"How long was Vince in the shed before he went back to the parking lot?"

"He didn't go back. He always parks his car down by the shed."

So the car with the headlights on in the parking lot belonged to somebody else.

"After Vince passed me on his way to the shed," Slim continued, "I seen him leaving in his own car, a black Maxima. There's a friggin' work road just beyond those trees."

Hmm. The greenskeeper could have been driving Al Jones's car, with his body in the trunk, parked it in the parking lot, then run to his own car, parked behind the shed.

"They were friends, weren't they—Vince Henry and Al Jones?"

"You kiddin'?" Slim scowled and lit another cigarette. "Al was always complainin' about the condition of the course."

"What about Vince?"

"Called Al a racist," Slim exhaled. "More than once."

"Did you hear any loud or bitter arguments between them?"

"You play golf, Detective? Then you know you're not allowed to yell. No one yells at this club. It's one of the biggest friggin' rules."

"You caddied for Al Jones?" I showed him the tournament photo from Jones's condo.

"I also clubbed him," Slim said, then grinned at his misspeak. "I don't mean upside his head. He wouldn'ta won without me. He was tied for the lead on the last hole. Gonna use a seven iron to bring it home, but I told him he needed every bit of a friggin' five. I coulda made it with a pitchin' wedge. I can hit the ball a country mile."

My five iron takes me about 175 yards. My seven's sharper blade angle and higher loft takes me 150. I only use my pitching wedge, with the sharpest angle and highest loft, when I'm much closer to the pin. I don't know about Al Jones, but Slim's dreaming if he thinks he can hit a pitching wedge a country mile.

"How did you know Jones needed a longer club?"

"He was gettin' tired from stayin' up too late the night before."

"Nerves?"

"A lady."

"How do you know?"

"Everyone knows. He coulda made the tour, but he always had one eye on the ball and the other on the gals in the gallery."

"This one maybe?" I indicated Mrs. O'Reilly in the photo.

"She took enough lessons—" Slim didn't just play good golf and caddy; he kept his eyes open.

A backdoor to the mansion behind us suddenly opened. The locker room attendant emerged with an armload of trash and tossed it into the garbage compactor. Slim and I turned to watch. If I had another question, I forgot it.

"Don't disappear," I told Slim, turning to leave.

"Can't I get nothin'?" he asked again.

I handed him a double sawbuck and advised, "Eat it, don't drink it."

Physician, heal thyself.

CHAPTER THIRTY-THREE

The greenskeeper's shed was a metal barn down a dirt work road, well away from Broken Oak's elysian fairways and beau monde. It looked unoccupied and locked, except for a partially open roll-up door about waist high. I ducked under it, like a limbo stick, pausing just inside to let my eyes adjust to the darkness. The only light came from two small air vents casting dusty shafts onto stacks of fertilizer bags from the roof peaks. The smell reminded me of the Staten Island landfill. Clusters of grass-cutting equipment reminded me that my own lawn was three feet high.

"Anybody here?" I called out across a stack of lime bags.

No answer.

I called out again, softer, for some strange reason.

Again no answer.

I looked behind a Locke mower, worried about Vince Henry leaping out at me like the charge of the Light Brigade, wondering if I should look for a light switch or continue probing the dead-grass gloom. Slipping between two tractors, I headed toward what looked like a shed within the shed. A storage room, tool room, toilet? I twisted the knob and pushed the door slowly open. No more calling out or knocking. I entered a small office, illuminated only by another air vent along an exterior wall, holding only a small, uncluttered desk with a swivel chair. A greenskeeper's desk should be messy, strewn with seed catalogs, odd tractor parts, broken pencils, grease-smudged receipts from irrigation vendors. A chest-high wooden shelf ringed the room, with tools placed carefully along its length like a museum display. Antique tools. Sturdy, hand-wrought, in excellent condition, made to last several lifetimes. Not like the plastic, disposable jobs in my workshop.

I hefted a hand-carved wooden block plane with a thick slab of steel for the blade and a solid brass adjustment lever. A tool made by and for craftsmen that would last forever. I felt its razor-sharp cutting edge, imagining the burly black greenskeeper shaving down the edge of a door, when someone suddenly behind me said, "They don't make 'em like that anymore."

I whirled to face Vince holding an antique scythe like the Grim Reaper, blocking the doorway. I wished the block plane I was holding was a Glock.

"They don't make scythes that size either," I said, hoping to draw a laugh, and my gun, before he cut me to shreds.

"Scythes count," Vince grinned, raising the terrible triangular blade like a devil's phallus. "I can cut a section of rough quicker and easier with this than with any of my tractors," he added.

"It looks awfully heavy," I said, hoping the notion of weight might slow him down.

"Needs to be," he said, "for cutting tall weeds and sawgrass. Balance is perfect," he continued, hefting the hideous tool and stepping toward me.

My free hand went for my gun, but he only shoved the scythe at me and said, with a smile, "Try it."

Breathing a sigh of relief, putting back the block plane, I took the tool.

"Swings easy," he said, adjusting his black baseball cap with the big white X on the crown.

"Sure does," I said, hoping my hands weren't shaking. How well does Vince swing a five iron?

"Made in the late 1700s," he informed me, like a museum tour guide. "Treat it right, it's good for a few more centuries. My great-grandfather used one just like it."

"I don't suppose he was a greenskeeper?" I said.

"He was a slave on a Georgia plantation who finally bought his freedom," said Vince, studying my reaction.

Good for him. My great-grandfather slaved his life away on a barren farm back in the old country. He bought the farm, so to speak, during the potato famine.

"You collect all these tools?" I said, indicating the surrounding shelves, keeping my own ignoble ancestry to myself.

"Still use them on occasion," Vince said, "including the one you're holding."

He unzipped his black windbreaker, smiling warily, still suspecting that I had some racial ax to grind. I could see him cutting down mountains of rough, and/or golfers who got in his way, with his great-grandfather's slave scythe. Like John Henry beating the steam drill, with a touch of Nat Turner, making a Black Power statement more effectively than did the big X on his baseball cap.

"Where were you last night?" I asked, now that *I* held the weapon.

"When the golf pro was murdered?"

I nodded.

"You think I killed the man?" He looked weary. "Okay, Detective. I was home."

I set the scythe in a corner, away from Vince. I wanted to keep holding it, but it was getting heavy.

"Where's your car?" I asked.

"Right by the barn."

"I didn't see it when I came in."

"Just drove up. You didn't hear me?"

"You're a lot smarter than that big X on your baseball cap indicates," I commented. "You said Mr. O'Reilly told you it was your IQ in Roman numerals."

"He also told me that Black Power is prune juice. But I wouldn't bother to kill him."

"Someone saw you here around the time Jones was murdered."

"Who?"

"You parked your car in the main lot and ran all the way down here for some reason."

"It was Slim told you, wasn't it? He's always here, drunker 'n a skunk. Passed out cold in that caddy shack."

"You deny that he saw you?"

"I work hard all day, Detective. 'Specially in the summer. I'm too damn tired at night to be haulin' dead bodies around and dumpin' 'em into trunks."

"You're a powerful man. You must have been a hell of a football player."

"You're not as dumb as you look either." Vince laughed. "But you can't flatter me into confessing. I was home all night. I got witnesses."

"My witness also says that Jones was always complaining about the condition of the course and blaming you for it."

"And Massa O'Reilly didn't like my baseball cap wit' dis big-ass X on it. Need a conviction, grab the nearest black man. You cops are all the same."

"You telling me Slim was hallucinating? You telling me you didn't run by him?"

"You takin' the word of a drunk, homeless cracker? I can't even call him trailer trash." Vince seemed to be getting bigger and looming larger every minute.

"You don't have to answer any of my questions."

"I know," the greenskeeper scoffed. "I got my rights and a seat on whitey's bus."

"You can also get a seat in my car on the way to headquarters."

"No need, Detective." The big man removed his cap, wiping some sweat from his brow. "Me and Al Jones butted heads on occasion, but I didn't kill the dude."

"Reseeding?" I asked.

"Say what?" He quickly replaced the cap, as though I meant his hair.

"You know. The grass out there."

"Oh, that. I'm always reseeding. Back nine, mostly. Ain't been much rain, and the watering system's not working perfect."

"It must be easier with the course closed."

"Tell me about it. No clowns drivin' their carts onto the greens and all over the ground I got under repair."

"Clowns like Mr. O'Reilly?"

"But you don't kill a man for that kind of shit," Vince scoffed.

"It only takes a fit of rage, a lapse in sanity."

"So you grab the nearest black man?"

"Show me where you've been reseeding before the grass grows back and hides the evidence."

I made sure he carefully stored the scythe before we left. It was then I noticed dozens of broken golf clubs stacked in a corner behind the door.

"Part of your antique tool collection?" I stopped to look at them—fives, threes, drivers, and so on. Golf is an expensive game if you don't take care of your clubs.

"They ain't old enough."

"They all broken?"

"The members beat 'em to death and leave 'em out on the course. Rage ain't exclusive to us black folks."

"Believe it or not," I said, "no one understands that better than us cops. But why save the busted clubs?"

The greenskeeper shrugged and said, "I keep them as a reminder to keep my head when I get frustrated. See how some of the heads are missing? When you lose your head, it's all over." He smiled at me as if I were close to flying off the handle.

"Any five irons?"

"Sure."

"Don't touch them."

"Why not? My prints are already all over them. Anyway, they didn't kill nobody," the greenskeeper insisted. "They been doing nothing but collecting dust in that corner for quite a while."

"We'll see," I said. "Now show me where you've been reseeding."

CHAPTER THIRTY-FOUR

"Zoysia, zoysia, zoysia," Vince Henry chanted, leading me like a native guide along fairways wider than the Serengeti.

"What's zoysia?" I asked, worried it was some voodoo chant or an incantation in Ebonics.

"Good grass," he said.

"The kind you smoke?"

"That's ganja."

"Tell me the truth about zoysia grass."

"It grows in quick and thick. Good for ground repair. And it's tough stuff."

"How long before it takes root and turns into the green stuff?"

" 'Bout a week, but it's fragile at first. I always rope off the area under repair, but some idiots still can't stay off."

"Like Mr. O'Reilly?" I said.

"Yeah," said the greenskeeper, immense shoulders tensing, eyes narrowing. I pictured him on the football field, mowing down the competition. Now he's mowing the zoysia.

We followed a cart path to the fifteenth fairway, way out on the course. I couldn't see the clubhouse or recognize any landmarks. I was lost.

"Over here," the greenskeeper said, heading toward a brown section of grass near a rocky little creek that could swallow your ball like Jaws, cordoned off with stakes and twine. The area reminded me of the outlines around the corpse forensics makes at a murder scene.

"When did you put this down?"

"Two days ago."

"It hasn't been watered?"

"I told you, the sprinkler system ain't workin' right." Vince looked as if he could strangle the waterworks with his bare hands.

"Don't water it," I said. "I want forensics to look at it first."

"Find any seeds on Jones's body?" Vince asked.

"I'll ask the questions," I reminded him.

This guy's pretty smart. O'Reilly ridiculing his IQ must have gnawed his innards, like a poisonous mineral, and the golf pro criticizing his care of the course wouldn't have pleased the big bruiser, either.

"You did more than get high in college," I said.

"Had to get through," said Vince, "after my knees blew out."

"No more football must have bothered you. But now you got a job in the real world."

"You kiddin', Detective? Broken Oak, and this part of Long Island for that matter, ain't the real world."

CHAPTER THIRTY-FIVE

I had to play golf. I couldn't bear hanging around Broken Oak without my clubs any longer. If only I could play there. But just imagine the flak if Randy Randall or a member caught me. Eisenhower Park public links in East Meadow, where you don't need big bucks and a pedigree, only thirty beans and a Nassau County leisure pass, would have to do. I also needed a break. Why not? It was Sunday, my day off, and Enrique Mendoza, aka Ricky, a fellow cop I had played with for years, had a tee-off time.

Walking off the eighteenth green, I grudgingly told Ricky, who had won almost every hole, "You played pretty well."

"Thanks, Karl." Ricky grinned.

"For a wetback," I added. Ricky and I had come up through the ranks together, until he made sergeant and I made detective. He likes his blue uniform, but he also lives in Bayville.

Ricky laughed and told me, "You wouldn't talk to Lee Trevino like that."

"You don't play like Super Mex," I reminded him.

"You don't play out of the water," Ricky said. "You take a drop and two strokes."

"I wasn't in that deep," I said. "I thought I could make a Royal Navy." That's a par after hitting into a water hazard.

"You made a submarine," said Ricky, "and lost the ball."

"I made that Woodie," I told him. A par after hitting a tree. I hardly ever hit a tree, but my hook has gotten worse since Carol died. "It kicked off that big sycamore," I added, "just like I planned it."

Ricky laughed again and said, "You should call it a Lumberjack, the way it kicked down that limb and most of the bark."

"Don't worry. I'm still buyin'," I said, wondering if I should skip the nineteenth hole. To civilians, the clubhouse bar.

"I'm only worried about the word around headquarters." Ricky put an arm around my shoulders. "They say you're goin' soft."

"They're wrong." I could wring Kowalski's neck.

"Only if you solve the Broken Oak murders, amigo."

"Thanks for reminding me." This has been a bad day and it's getting worse.

"How long we been playin' together?"

"Since the game was invented. And this is the first time you ever beat me. Remember?" I was getting a headache.

"Oh, I get it. You're joining Broken Oak?" He laughed like a hyena.

"Don't be ridiculous. You know my salary and social position."

"Don't I know, amigo. I couldn't get in if I was Chi Chi Rodriguez."

"What about Tiger Woods?"

"He could be a caddy, maybe."

"And you could be a busboy."

"I hear they wait on you hand and foot over there," Ricky said longingly. "They even polish your balls for you."

As we stowed our bags in our cars, I said, "Imagine always finding a parking space, unlike this place that's always packed, and waltzing up to the first tee, where the starter's always smiling and you haven't sold your soul for a half-decent time, where the tees haven't been hacked to death, the fairways don't remind you of Death Valley, and the greens are to die for, not moribund."

"Where the locker room is nicer than my living room?"

"With clean, fluffy towels. As many as you want."

"I found a clean towel here last week, about the size of a taco shell and twice as hard."

"That reminds me. Where's the Desenex I loaned you?"

"I used it up. The microbes in the locker rooms we frequent crawl over you like cucarachas. *Madre mia*, some are bigger than my fist. Even in the steam rooms, where all living organisms, including us if we stay too long, should be dead as doornails."

"You love these places." I put my arm around Ricky's shoulders. "They're cheap."

"Bet there's no microbes at Broken Oak."

"But one of their members *and* the golf pro are dead as doornails."

We entered the locker room, stripped off our sweaty clothes, and headed for the showers.

"You still pissed about losing?" Ricky asked. "I figure your head wasn't into it."

"I've been told I don't use my head for anything."

"Captain Kowalski?"

"And Gleason."

"Gleason's okay. And at least you're still in shape," Ricky said, as we stepped into the showers and turned them on.

"I'm not so sure anymore," I said.

"I could lose a few pounds since taking the desk job," Ricky added. "Golf's not doing it for me. I need more exercise."

"You need to cut back on the quesadillas."

"That reminds me, amigo. Want to come for dinner?"

I shook my head, feeling too much pressure from the goings-on at Broken Oak to enjoy myself at dinner or on the golf course.

"If you don't mind my saying," Ricky said, "you've changed since Carol died. You used to love to come over."

"Nothing endures but change," I said, recalling an aphorism Carol often used. Ricky looked quizzical, and I added, "Heraclitus said that, not me."

"Oh, yeah. Jimmy Heraclitus. Owns the Glen Cove Diner."

"He was an ancient Greek philosopher, you oy-ay."

"Sounds pretty smart," Ricky said, like I'm not. "Too bad he can't help you catch your killer."

"Killers, maybe," I said. "I've got more suspects than wetbacks crossing the Rio Grande. But I can't find the murder weapon. I can't even find the spot where the golf pro got whacked. Forensics found a certain type of grass seed on him. I had them combing over all the spots where they'd recently seeded, but they also got nothing. The same seeds are everywhere. Zoysia."

"Zoysia? Don't tell me. He's an old Polack philosopher."

I smiled halfheartedly and continued, "I checked my suspects' lawns to see if they were recently reseeded. Dr. Fitch uses sod. Wouldn't you know? He doesn't have the patience to let grass grow, and his temper's hotter than a tamale from hell."

"What about O'Reilly?"

"No new seeds. There won't be any for a while. His property is in receivership. But Vince Henry, the Broken Oak greenskeeper, has seeds galore. He also had a motive for both murders and more than enough strength to whack a big guy like Al Jones and toss him into his trunk."

"I feel for you, amigo," said Ricky, shutting off his shower. "If you add that club manager to the mix, plus his fat cousin, you got a real rogues gallery."

"All I've got is a pair of golf shoes that match a heel print at the scene of the first murder," I said, shivering slightly. I'm pretty sure it was from the cold shower, not fear of falling flat on my face at Broken Oak, or missing Carol. "They're a common brand," I added. "There are hundreds of pairs in every golf outlet across the country, and they don't fit any of my suspects."

"You tried them all?"

"All except Dr. Fitch."

"Madre mia!" Ricky shrieked, as if he'd been scalded. "What're you waiting for? Slap those shoes on that hot tamale. Go for the hole. You always do, regardless of the lie."

"He is a good liar," I considered.

"Draw him out," Ricky advised, "like you draw the golf ball."

"When my game's not off?"

"You're always on," Ricky insisted. "You're a legend; the Walter Hagen of homicide. He won sixteen majors, including the PGA championship right here at Eisenhower."

"Thanks, Ricky," I said, feeling older than Arnold Palmer, "but that was back in 1926."

CHAPTER THIRTY-SIX

I had dinner alone at a Wendy's near Eisenhower Park. As alone as you can be at a busy fast-food restaurant. Maybe I should have gone to Ricky's, but getting invited to someone's home because they know you're lonely seems even lonelier.

The Wendy's was filled with an interesting cross section of American culture: plucky youngsters picking at kid's meals, mostly for the toys; heart attack candidates glomming triple cheeseburgers and biggie fries; biker types wearing black Bermudas, white socks, and wife beaters. There was also a group that was headed for a pro soccer game, ordering taco salads in Spanish.

I was more interested in *Murder on the Moor*, however, reading it while eating, admiring the way Peter H. Couloir continues to operate so smoothly, while I floundered like my fish sandwich. Wishing that I could sift the clues, synthesize the situation, take a step back and let the suspects hang themselves, like the Frenchie does. His intellect was scintillating and I was brain-dead.

I was reading the final chapter, with five remaining suspects: the evil earl of Cranbrook, his shady gamekeeper, his creepy butler, the snooty Lady Barkworth, the dynamite Mrs. Phelps. I was clueless as to the culprit, and how Couloir would crack the case, short of hauling them all into an anteroom and getting out the rubber hoses. What's brainpower over biceps, when gray matter is a gray area? Nonfictional killers, I know from experience, are always too desperate and dangerous to retire peacefully to a drawing room at the behest of some cerebral little detective and benignly announce, "Good show, old chap. You got me."

"I have gathered you here," Couloir murmured . . .

You lucky little stiff. There's not a drawing room at Broken Oak that's big enough for all my suspects.

". . . to expose the murderer . . ."

Colonel Mustard, in the kitchen, with a candestick?

". . . who is, at this very moment, among us."

This little tec's got big balls.

Quick glances were exchanged between the Earl, Lady Barkworth, and Mrs. Phelps. And between the gamekeeper and the butler. "This is most inconvenient," said Lady Barkworth.

Royalty's always been a pain in the butt.

"It's preposterous!" snapped the Earl.

"We shall see . . ."

Couloir's got the evil earl all figured out. It's about time. Now slap the cuffs on him and slap him silly.

"You did kill dear, sweet Esmond," Lady Barkworth reminded the Earl.

"That was entirely an accident," he said. "It's quite apparent that Uncle Esmond murdered both Phelps and Algie."

"How do you know?" asked Mrs. Phelps.

"He was holding the murder weapon," explained the Earl. "And he would have shot me, had I not overpowered him in our struggle."

"What was his motive?"

"He was quite deranged. Who could be certain? He never liked Americans, and old Algie may only have been in the wrong place at the wrong time, as I was."

"In one instance, monsieur, you are correct," said Couloir. "M. Spotswood merely stumbled onto the plot."

"Plot? What plot?" asked the Earl.

"There was indeed a plot," Couloir insisted. "And it was a most cleverly contrived one."

"Then by all means," said Lady Barkworth, "please enlighten us."

Yeah. Shove it up their aristocratic asses.

"You see," Couloir began, "we have learned that the Earl of Cranbrook owed M. Phelps a great deal of money, from some unfortunate business dealings."

"That was common knowledge," said the Earl. "Perhaps you are not so clever as your reputation would indicate."

Good-bye, earl. Never taunt a cop.

"We shall see," said Couloir, with more than a trace of self-confidence.

"He'd be a fool to have murdered him," Lady Barkworth offered.

Mrs. Phelps said, "But not to have put someone up to it."

I don't know. The earl's pretty good with that Webley-Vickers.

"Précisement, Madame," Couloir continued. "But the Earl was not the only one who would gain from your husband's untimely demise."

Suddenly seeming more respectful of Couloir's reputation, the Earl said, "Please do enlighten us, Detective."

"You, Mrs. Phelps, will no doubt inherit your husband's estate."

"And you, M. Couloir, are quite correct. However, I have enjoyed a very successful career in my own right, with no small remuneration."

I think she's saying she doesn't need the money.

"Indeed, I have enjoyed your performances at both La Scala and the Paris Opera."

On a cop's pay?

"Why, M. Couloir, thank you."

"Surely she did not shoot these two men," the Earl interceded.

"Why not?" asked Lady Barkworth.

The Earl explained, "The Webley .44 is an extremely powerful handgun. Its recoil is far too severe for a woman . . ."

This was written in the prefeminist era. I know more than a few females who can handle any weapon.

". . . and both Algie and Phelps were done in by perfectly placed shots through the center of the chest."

"I too had taken that into consideration," said Couloir. "Along with the fact that the lady's hands are very small and delicate. Most expressive hands, heartrending in fact as Mimi's in La Bohème, but incapable of handling such a volatile weapon."

"Again, M. Couloir, I thank you."

Turn her on, then turn her in?

"No, indeed," Couloir affirmed. "Mrs. Phelps did not shoot either of the two gentlemen in question. But she did put someone up to it."

"Why, M. Couloir," Mrs. Phelps said as though accepting another compliment, "whatever led such a great detective to such an absurd conclusion?"

"Your perfume, madame."

"What?"

"Eau de la Nuit, n'est-ce pas?"

"Yes, but why do you ask?"

"A lovely scent, with which I am quite familiar . . ."

Maybe you use it.

". . . delicate as a summer night's breeze off the Seine . . . it was in the room where the Earl struggled for the gun with Esmond.

I would have recognized it immediately were it not for all the con-fusion, noise, and the overwhelming smell of gunpowder . . ."

What about the aroma of Uncle Esmond's blood?

". . . you, Mrs. Phelps, were in that room only moments ear-lier, handing the gun to Esmond, convincing him that his nephew had gone mad, murdered your husband and M. Spotswood, and you were pleading with Esmond to halt the Earl's bloody ram-page, using the Webley, setting the stage, as it were, to look as if poor demented Esmond had murdered all three."

"Amusing scenario," said Mrs. Phelps. "You should write comic opera. But how did I gain possession of this horrible murder weapon?"

"It was given to you by your accomplice, who committed both murders. Who is"

Damn. Where's the last page?

CHAPTER THIRTY-SEVEN

I rushed home to search for that last page. I even looked in the fridge. I found a six-pack instead. Plus a stale loaf of bread, some cheese that's not normally green, and a box of Arm & Hammer baking soda Carol had put in more than a year ago. I tossed out the old food, tossed down a beer, and tried to relax with an idiot TV sitcom. I like *Drew Carey* but could not help thinking about that last page of *Murder on the Moor*. Is it in the basement, in that box of Carol's stuff, where I originally discovered the broken little book? I turned off the boob tube and descended into the sepulcher for a look.

No page. Only scads of Carol's stuff I still can't throw out. Or even sift through. Just looking at it devastates me. I went back upstairs and popped the top of another cold one. "Of all the friends in time of grief, when threatening death looks grimmer, not one so sure can bring relief as this best friend, a brimmer." I like that toast from an old play my wife begged me to see with her. I forget the title. Something about an opera. Written by a gay guy. The toast was the only part worth a damn.

After my fifth or so brimmer, I lost count. *Murder on the Moor*, the play by the gay guy, and the murders at Broken Oak blurred. In my state, nothing made sense. There seemed to be no reason since the Age of Reason. No enlightenment since the Age of Enlightenment. No information in this so-called Information Age, except easy online gun buying and A-bomb recipes. Artificial intelligence is displacing little gray cells, common sense, gut feeling.

Gut feeling's my only strength, in lieu of merely average gray matter. And a bottle of Bud is as good a muse as a fine Bordeaux. At least I don't need fancy bar concoctions, like pousse cafés or perfect martinis, to create case-breaking insights. No one makes a perfect pousse café, anyway, or cares to drink it. And a perfect martini's merely a glass of gin.

I stopped drinking and sat at the kitchen table, jotting down possible scenarios for the Broken Oak murders on a pad Carol used for grocery lists. First, Randy Randall could have murdered O'Reilly for threatening to buy Broken Oak, raze Dame Winifred's historic mansion, and slap condos all over the property. But Randall could have checked O'Reilly's finances and found he was flat broke. Or, and this is stretching it, Randy could also have been in love with Mrs. O and was killing two birds with one stone. And she could have put him up to it, having the looks, charm, and brains not to do the dirty work herself. Then Randall murdered Al Jones as a cover-up when Jones stumbled onto their plot, or witnessed the murder, and demanded blackmail or threatened to turn them in. Randall did seem overly protective of Mrs. O when I noticed she was signed up for so many golf lessons. He could also have whacked Jones out of jealousy.

Second, the terrible-tempered Dr. Fitch could have killed O'Reilly over the money he owed him. Or maybe he'd played a bad round and simply had to take it out on somebody. Even if the shoes with the missing heel spike fit him, however, it proves nothing.

Third, Randy Randall's fatso cousin Gregory murdered O'Reilly to protect the property and save the mansion. He had to have been outside; otherwise, where had he gotten all those golf balls under his cot? He could have a crush on Mrs. O, figuratively speaking, adoring her from his window behind the spires and gargoyles. Like Quasimodo and Esmeralda, longingly watching her take lesson after lesson from the tall Texan. But isn't he too heavy and slow to whack anyone?

Fourth, Slim killed O'Reilly for being a lousy tipper. Maybe Jones stiffed him after caddying in that tournament he won. Murder most foul is committed for much less.

Fifth, Vince Henry killed O'Reilly for the Malcolm X IQ comment. Then he whacked Jones for criticizing the way the greens were cut.

Sixth, but certainly not last, the enigmatic Mrs. O put her lover, Jones, up to killing her husband. Then she whacked him with the swing he'd helped her to perfect. The *Enquirer* would love that bit of irony.

Fuzzy and frustrated, I put the list aside, grabbed another beer, and wandered outside, like O'Reilly at his last cocktail party. Instead of heading for a water hazard to empty my bladder, however, I walked to the small graveyard along Bayville Avenue where Carol was buried. I visited her, even though she wouldn't like seeing me loaded and lachrymose.

I poured some beer onto one of the graves, intoning, "To quench the fire of anguish in some eye, there hidden far beneath and long ago." Omar Khayyam said that. I used to tell my wife it was really Omar Kanopka, a Polack rug dealer and distant relative from Perth Amboy. I still think it's funny, though I know too many toasts and have had too many cocktail parties alone lately.

I sat beside Carol's grave in the darkness. I didn't dare pour a drop in her memory, but I dropped a few tears. I dropped my empty beer can into a trash barrel on the way out. Let the grave digger get the nickel deposit. I wandered along Bayville Avenue, where my tenants waved as they drove past while I tried to look sober. I watched them turn into my driveway. I could almost hear them laughing and clamoring out of their car, groping and fondling each other as they climbed the outside stairs to their apartment. More than ever, I wished they were my kids.

I walked past the Renaissance Adult Home, where I pray I'll never have to stay. Bury me next to my wife before I'm infirm and senile, with fresh breezes off the Sound and someone, even if it's only the grave digger, occasionally pouring a drop on my grave.

I passed the restaurant called Steve's Pier. It was busy and noisy as always. The food's great, but I'd prefer pablum at the Renaissance Adult Home to five-pound lobsters amid clusters of clamoring yuppies with cell phones.

I also passed a homey little deli, closed for the night, and several small shops, including the all-night Laundromat where I occasionally wash my clothes. Not because my washing machine at home is broken, but because I have to get out of the house and be with people, away from solitary cocktail parties.

Passing the Laundromat, I glanced through the plate glass front window, hoping to recognize someone, if only to wave. It was past midnight, but lonely souls in Bayville are soaping and rinsing at all hours. I never expected to see

Mrs. O'Reilly, alone and leaning into one of the dryers. She was poured into a pair of faded jeans, obviously braless under a thin cotton T-shirt. My beer buzz faded like her jeans as I suddenly recalled that the Black Widow and I were neighbors, that she's still at the Tides Motel, only a short walk from here.

As she took an armload of clothes from the dryer, I stared through the plate glass like a peeper. Her looks and the realization that killers also do laundry were captivating. She saw me and waved, smiling as if it were old home week, and she's not a prime suspect.

"You staking me out?" she asked, when I moved to the Laundromat's open front door.

"I live up the street," I admitted.

"So you've told me."

"Just getting some air," I said, staying outside, keeping my beer breath with me.

"Cops also need air," she sighed, folding her laundry.

Had I misread her? Like *Murder on the Moor*? Misapplying a seemingly similar murder plot between her and Randy Randall?

I could not help saying, "Like killers need clean clothes?"

"Don't look," she said, ignoring the comment and folding a lacy pair of panties, similar to the ones in the sand trap with the condom. Could I snare a pair without her taking me for a fetishist?

"They're pretty," I said, stepping inside.

"Pretty personal," she told me, tucking them under a sweatshirt she'd already folded.

Women are amazing. You catch them in their birthday suits and they don't so much as blush. You accuse them of murder and they become concerned about hiding their underwear.

"Gotta go," I told her, giving up on my panty raid. They looked pretty average without Mrs. O in them, and dryers kill DNA.

"Too bad." She feigned a pout. Like a prizefighter feints, then jabs?

"But don't you go anywhere," I warned.

"Can you give me a hand before you go?" she asked, stacking her folded clothes to overflowing in a large laundry basket.

Watch it, Kanopka. This could be a sucker punch.

"Where's your car?" I asked.

I saw myself placing the laundry basket in her trunk, while she raised a five iron behind me.

"I walked here," she said, hoisting the heavy basket like a feather. "I don't need any help with this, but you could carry the bleach and this detergent. I kept dropping them on the way here."

Was she strong enough to have whacked Al Jones and hoisted him into his trunk? I took the bleach and detergent, knowing only that she's good-looking enough to get anyone to do her dirty work, including me, when I should be arresting her.

Her room at the Tides was tidy. Why had I thought it would be a mess?

"Put them on the dresser," she said, setting her laundry basket on the bed, putting away the clean clothes.

I did not take my eyes off her, partly because she's pretty and partly because she *could* whip out a five iron.

"Gotta go," I repeated. "It's getting late."

"But I owe you something for your help."

"You owe me nothing but the truth," I lectured her in full detective mode.

"I've told you the truth."

"Then we're even."

"Truth is, I have a good bottle of Scotch I don't want to drink by myself."

"Well . . ."

The last thing I needed was another drink, or getting drunk with a murder suspect. I felt I staggered a bit on the short walk from the Laundromat to the Tides.

"A short one," I said, "but that's all."

She produced a bottle of Chivas Regal, two of the motel's plastic cups, and ice from its plastic bucket.

"You must miss your house," I said, as she poured. "There's not much room in here."

"I'm used to small spaces," she shrugged. "I grew up in Levittown, in a house the size of a cracker box."

You could buy a new Levit house, including a new TV set, for about four thousand bucks in the 1940s. Now those cracker boxes cost a fortune.

"But I'm not used to plastic cups for Chivas on the rocks," she added, handing me one.

"Good Scotch is good Scotch," I said inanely, wondering if my little gray cells were also on the rocks.

"Skoal," she said, sounding like a native Swede, touching our cups.

"Salut," I said, reminding myself that I wasn't French and was still on duty. Cops are always on duty and shouldn't flirt with murder suspects.

"I have a confession," said Mrs. O.

"After one sip of Scotch?" I said. This is a great interrogation method.

"I stole my husband's last bottle of Chivas from the house when I left. It's the only thing I wanted, besides my clothes."

Now confess to killing him. I felt sick at the thought.

"You going to arrest me?"

"Too late. You've opened the bottle, tampered with the evidence."

She laughed, as if our little tête-à-tête had nothing to do with murder.

"How did you meet your husband?" I said, changing the subject before my testosterone took over from the little gray cells.

"I worked at an indoor tennis club near Roosevelt Field," she said. "Receptionist and secretary."

"Your husband played there?"

"He never played tennis."

"Really?"

"I'm a pretty good player," she said, putting down her cup, showing me the motion for her backhand. "But my husband didn't know which end of the racquet to hold. Ugh! He built the facility. And you'll love this. His court construction crew lined all the service boxes three feet short."

"Were they drunk?" I asked, wishing I could show her my golf swing.

"I don't know, but the players must have been. It was weeks before anyone noticed. Even the pros. My husband and his company were long gone by then, so the owners had to pay for the error."

"Developers can get away with murder," I said, reminded of the problems Ricky Mendoza had with building his new house. But Ricky didn't kill his developer, and O'Reilly didn't kill himself.

"It was typical of his projects," Mrs. O added. "That building leaked like a sieve, the heating and plumbing never worked."

Picturing her husband's diminutive plumbing on the autopsy table, I asked, "You knew all that before you married him?"

"He seemed so in control," Mrs. O told me, retrieving her cup, "despite any mistakes and shortcomings. He gambled and mostly he won. I guess he snowed me."

"He had the gift of gab?" I asked, though I already knew the answer.

"He could sell iceboxes to Eskimos," she assured me. "He was also a drunk, and he chased anything in skirts."

"So you murdered him?" I said, cutting to the chase, and cutting my Chivas with a shot of tap water from a small sink beside the dresser.

"You're murdering great Scotch," she said.

"You put Al Jones up to it," I said, "then murdered him to keep him quiet because you were having an affair."

"I've already told you," said Mrs. O, "I only took golf lessons."

"Okay, were you having an affair with Randy Randall?"

"Why not both of them? Surely you've heard of it. It's called a club sandwich. And throw in three board members for good measure."

I tried not to smile as I finished my drink and tossed the remaining ice into the sink.

"Another?" she asked, like a black widow spider enticing me into her web.

"Gotta go," I told her. "Forensics will have some answers for me early in the morning."

Don't I wish? But maybe this will give her pause.

"One for the road won't hurt," she insisted.

"Thanks, but—"

"Please stay," she whispered, drawing close, initiating the first kiss.

CHAPTER THIRTY-EIGHT

Mrs. O was asleep when I left her at dawn the next morning. Now I can call her Mrs. O, for orgasm, unless she was faking it. Was she also faking sleep? The sleep of the innocent? At least she did not try convincing me of her innocence during our lovemaking, though she did try convincing me that I'm a good lover.

I'm not proud of shtupping my prime suspect, but neither am I worried about the serious breach of procedure. Who cares if I'm brought up on charges, tossed off the case, summarily canned? I only hope that Carol understands I can't sit at home alone counting flowers on the wall forever.

I walked back home along Bayville Beach. The early morning sun was a tsunami of light, cresting tall trees behind the Tides, roaring across the Sound to inundate Connecticut. I wished I could have lingered with Mrs. O. Maybe we could have made love again. At least we could have had a leisurely breakfast together, as I often did with Carol. The late Mrs. K. Now the initials of my only two lovers are OK. Okay. I married early and never got around much.

Passing back by the little graveyard where my wife is buried was definitely not okay. Somehow, I could not look in as usual to make sure that her grave was tidy, the headstone untoppled, graffiti-free. I held my breath and hurried toward my house, like a superstitious kid caught in a misdemeanor.

I had barely caught my breath when I lost it again. Why were two patrol cars parked in my driveway? I had no burglar alarm to go off accidentally. Not even a car alarm. Nothing to steal, anyway. Did the young couple upstairs turn their first argument into a civil dispute? Did they play their stereo too loud? Did an envious neighbor dime them out for having an orgasm equivalent to an earthquake?

"There he is!" a uniformed cop shouted.

"What's wrong?" I called back, dashing up my driveway.

"Where you been, Detective?"

"Never mind where I've been! What the hell's going on?"

"We got another stiff."

"One of the kids?" I sprinted for the outside stairs to their apartment.

"Not here." The uniform stopped me.

"Where?"

"Over at Broken Oak."

CHAPTER THIRTY-NINE

Randy Randall's cousin Gregory lay like a beached whale in the middle of the sixth fairway. An idyllic par four, with the morning sun poking through the trees and carefully planted fountain grasses swaying in the breeze, except for Moby Dick lying where I'd surely hit my tee shot. The ME was examining him, with Captains Gleason and Kowalski looking on. Randall, Vince Henry, and Slim the caddy were cordoned away from the scene with several others. My entire list of suspects, except for Dr. Fitch and Mrs. O. At least I knew the latter did not commit this one.

"Nice of you to join us," Kowalski smirked.

"What happened?" I said.

"They don't know yet," said Gleason.

"No apparent marks on the body," the ME said. "It could have been a heart attack."

That seemed logical, but I suspected foul play. That's what I get paid for. The corpse was also clutching a five iron, with a line of golf balls leading away from it. Was he dropping the balls, walking or running, trying to leave a trail or some kind of sign?

I looked closely at the five iron and said, "Looks like ashes on the blade."

Randall, Slim, and the greenskeeper were beyond hearing distance.

"That could be significant," the ever cautious ME admitted, "if they match the ashes we found in the head wounds of the others."

"Is that dried blood on the shaft?" I asked, squinting at a few brownish specs.

"Most likely," the ME said.

"Looks like mud," said Kowalski.

"I know blood when I see it," the ME said.

"When will you know if it belongs to O'Reilly or Al Jones?" I asked.

"That takes more time," the ME told me, as if I didn't know.

"Wonder what prints are on it?" Kowalski said.

"You think this guy murdered Jones and O'Reilly?" Gleason asked me.

"Maybe the five iron was planted on him," I said.

"Or he could have found it."

"While looking for golf balls?"

"He had a hell of a collection."

"Come on, Kanopka. He's your killer," Kowalski said. "You're lucky he had a heart attack or you'd never have caught him."

"What makes you so certain?" I said.

"He's holding the murder weapon," Kowalski shrugged. "With those ashes on it and blood from one or both victims. Case closed."

"Nice and clean," Gleason concurred. "They should all end this way. No long, drawn-out trials at the taxpayers' expense."

"Where killers become media stars," Kowalski added, "at the expense of victims and their families."

"Where everyone loses except the lawyers?" I said, warily.

"And good cops like you, Karl." Kowalski grinned, suddenly friendly.

"Cops who get stuck between the proverbial rock and the hard place," Gleason added, also grinning.

These two are up to something. They're also under extreme pressure to solve these murders because there's enough big bucks and political clout at Broken Oak to kick serious cop butt. A long, drawn-out trial would wreck the club's reputation and expose members to media scrutiny and abuse. The fix is obviously in, whether Randall's obese cousin is the killer or not. The bottom line, I realized as suddenly as Kowalski had become friendly, is not to inconvenience these pillars of the community and keep creeps like Dr. Fitch off the golf course for too long.

"What was Gregory's motive?" I asked.

"That's easy," Kowalski said, expanding his chest. "He wanted to keep O'Reilly's development cartel from taking over this property and demolishing the mansion."

"There was no such animal," I told him. "O'Reilly was flat broke."

"This guy didn't know it," Kowalski scoffed.

"He'd never even seen O'Reilly," I objected.

"Maybe he saw O'Reilly's picture in the club newsletter," Gleason said, "or that newspaper clipping you found in Jones's condo."

"That's it." Kowalski nodded, like a bobble-head doll.

"What are you two doing?" I asked. You shits.

"What do you mean?" the captains said, almost in unison.

"You sound like lawyers for the prosecution," I said. Which politico's got you in his pocket?"

"Why are you defending this blubber bag?" Gleason said.

"Yeah," said Kowalski. "It's an open-and-shut case."

"I know this guy lying here," I said.

"Sure," said Kowalski. "You and Richard Simmons."

"I'm no diet and exercise guru," I said, "but I do know that he only cared about his golf ball collection."

"Not his next meal?" Kowalski queried.

"Take it easy, you two," Gleason scowled. "We all know there's plenty of disturbed persons who'll commit murder."

"Then why did he whack Al Jones?"

"Easy," Kowalski said. "Jones somehow knew he knocked off O'Reilly."

"How?"

"The golf shoes."

"But they don't fit him. Or Jones. Or any other suspects."

"They all tried them on?"

"All except Dr. Fitch," I admitted.

"Forget about him," Gleason's eyes narrowed. Fitch must make one hell of a contribution to the PBA.

"Yeah," Kowalski insisted. "This guy did it. He had the motive and he's holding the murder weapon."

"You really believe that this man, who couldn't run the length of this golf ball trail without dropping dead, whacked a big guy like Jones and single-handedly dumped him into the trunk of his car?"

The captains looked at each other and shrugged simultaneously. Kowalski said, "Why not?"

Gleason walked away.

"Leave it, for Christ's sake," Kowalski told me under his breath. "It's neat and it's clean."

"You call this clean?" The fat cousin was a mess. His face was contorted, his pants were fouled, and his shirt was untucked, displaying a huge belly and more stretch marks than a woman eight months pregnant with quints.

"This case is closed, Kanopka. Forget it."

"I can't."

"Listen to me, Karl. Not like I'm your captain, but like a kumpel."

"When did you become my Polack pal?"

"Where were *you* last night?"

"I was home."

"You weren't home this morning." He had something on his mind and I wasn't going to like it.

"I was out for my morning constitutional."

"At the Tides Motel?"

"I couldn't sleep."

"I think you did. To put it politely, I think you slept over last night with Mrs. O'Reilly."

"You son of a bitch."

"Watch it. I got rank here. And get this through your thick Polack head," Kowalski poked my chest with his middle finger. "If this guy's not our killer and the case goes to trial, your conduct last night, or call it your morning constitutional, means you're finished as a cop and facing possible felony charges."

I pushed his hand away, but he continued reading me the riot act.

"If your Mrs. O'Reilly had anything to do with these murders, any defense attorney will have a field day with you on the witness stand. Even the prosecution can't ignore your misconduct. You could even be charged as an accomplice."

I should never have slept with Mrs. O, and let down my guard. I deserve this rebuke, though it's tough to take from Kowalski.

"Don't be ridiculous," I said, feeling like a fool.

"Don't become the butt of another Polack joke," said Kowalski, "just because you refused to close the case and got yourself convicted."

"So it's still my case?"

"As long as you clean it up with this." Kowalski nodded at the corpse.

"Or else?"

"Or else, kumpel, I'll teach you not to defy my authority, stick your nose where it's not wanted and fuck your suspects."

CHAPTER FORTY

K owalski's threat was compelling, but it's tough tossing the head detective off a murder case. Even if he's not your kumpel, it makes the brass look bad for assigning him in the first place.

"It was bound to happen," Randy Randall told me, as forensics loaded his cousin into the meat wagon. I hoped he didn't hear them complaining they didn't go to med school to get hernias. I almost felt sorry for him. His sallow pallor and the bags under his eyes made him look like he hadn't slept in a week.

"What do you mean?" I said, not sorry that Gleason and Kowalski had gone back to headquarters.

"He was always raiding the refrigerators," Randall said, resignedly. "He once ate fifty *mousses au chocolat* we had prepared for a wedding reception."

"Your dessert chef murdered him?"

"Hardly." Randall clenched his teeth. "But *I* could have killed him."

"When did he do this?"

"Late at night."

"Aren't the refrigerators locked?" I said.

"He found a key or picked the locks," said Randall. "He was very clever."

"Wait a minute. A few days ago, you portrayed him as being incapable of doing anything but stuffing his face and collecting lost golf balls." Gotcha!

"I was merely observing that he could not, or would not, have murdered anyone. I suppose I was wrong." The normally natty Randy looked disheveled; shirt wrinkled, trousers uncreased, shoelaces untied.

"You also told me he never saw O'Reilly or Al Jones. Not even in a photograph?"

"I believe not."

"You could have given Gregory a good description of O'Reilly."

"You think I put him up to it?" Randall squatted and started tying his shoelaces.

"You had reason enough," I told him.

"To murder O'Reilly, maybe. But why would I want my golf pro dead?" Randall thought a moment while he finished tying and then said, "The shoe should have been on the other foot. He should have wanted me dead."

"Why?"

"I fired him." He stood and faced me again.

"When?"

"The week before. Effective Labor Day."

"Now you tell me?"

"It's not unusual," Randall said offhandedly. "Golf pros are used to it. They're a peripatetic lot."

"And you were also pissed that he was having an affair with Mrs. O'Reilly."

"Of that, I'm not certain." He actually did look dubious. His eyebrows furrowed, accentuating the bags under his eyes.

"Then I suggest you tell me, right now, exactly what it is you *are* certain about."

"What good would it do? You've got your killer, holding the smoking golf club, so to speak. Let the healing process begin, Detective. Let Broken Oak get back to normal, if possible, with a modicum of dignity." He should have been an undertaker.

Nice try, but it won't work. I bet you gave Gleason and Kowalski the same speech, but I'm not buying it. It's time to get tough, with at least a verbal wham-bam.

"Withholding evidence in a murder case is a felony," I told him. "Your dignity, along with your sweet behind, could be sorely compromised in prison."

"I've been quite cooperative," Randall insisted, stiffly, unperturbed by the threat of prison intimacy. "You and your men have had the run of the place. I need to open the course and the restaurant again, or these beautiful grounds *will* ultimately fall prey to the bulldozers. Broken Oak needs healing and closure."

"Excellent choice of words. I'll keep this place closed as long as I want. Unless you tell me who Jones was screwing."

I could see the wheels spinning inside Randall's head. My threat, though a total bluff, seemed to be working.

"If you insist," Randall finally said. "I have reason to believe that Al Jones was seeing Mrs. Fitch."

CHAPTER FORTY-ONE

"You cops made a mess," Vince Henry grumbled as he tidied up the sixth fairway, raking and disposing of coffee cups and doughnut boxes. I thought he was going to pull out a portable vacuum cleaner and give the area some serious housekeeping.

"Next time," I quipped, "I'll slap us with summonses for littering."

"Won't be no next time, Detective. You got your killer."

That's what they're saying.

I studied the golf ball trail apparently left by Gregory. The balls, now little flags placed by forensics, were spaced approximately the same distance apart, almost in a straight line. As if dropped systematically. By a homicidal maniac on the dead run? Or a fat guy having a heart attack? Not likely.

Running beside the trail of flags, I dropped several golf balls I had found elsewhere, releasing them as carefully as possible to achieve straightness and equidistance. But the little buggers rolled all over the place. Like most of my golf shots.

"Tryin' out for the Olympics?" Vince said, looking like I'd flipped.

"Someone running couldn't have done this," I said, indicating the flags, flapping in the breeze like banners inspiring my defeat.

"His balls would be all over the place," the greenskeeper grinned.

We laughed, man to man. Balls have no racial boundaries.

"How come you find all the bodies out here?" I asked. "Maybe they should call you the cryptkeeper."

"Occupational hazard," he shrugged.

"But you haven't told me all you know," I said, ignoring the fact that more cops die in the line of duty than greenskeepers. "You're the only one who's out here all the time," I added.

"Tell me about it, Detective." The boundaries were back up.

"You know who drives their carts onto the greens, who fails to replace their divots, and who so much as farts."

"All I know is two guys got their skulls busted, the fat dude had a heart attack, and you leveled my fountain grass lookin' for evidence." The tall clumps of decorative grasses adorning the sides of the fairway were somewhat the worse for wear, but that shouldn't bother him more than murder.

"All I know," I shot back, "is that you're full of shit."

"Say what?" The greenskeeper clenched his big fists.

"You heard me." I stepped close to the burly ex–football player, sizing him up, considering the extensive damage he could do to me.

"I told you all I know," he said. "What else do you want? You already got your killer."

"He's no killer. He was running away from the killer."

"But he was holdin' the murder weapon," Vince insisted. "I saw it myself. I also heard your medical examiner."

"It could have been planted," I told him, stepping even closer, ready to duck if necessary.

"I get it." Vince glared at me. "I do a lot of planting out here. Is that what you're tellin' me? All this grass, these bushes and shit. I chased him down and planted that five iron on him."

"You also collect old golf clubs."

"But I wasn't chasin' the fat dude. I woulda caught him before he croaked."

"And?"

"He woulda looked a lot different."

"I thought your knees were bad."

"So were O.J.'s."

CHAPTER FORTY-TWO

I studied Al Jones's appointment book again. I had been so excited about Mrs. O's many lessons that I had ignored Mrs. Fitch. Her first lesson was back in March. Jones had just arrived from Texas. Unlike Mrs. O, however, Mrs. Fitch was penciled in for only one a week. Slow and steady. The smart way to cover up an affair.

I kicked myself for not considering that a woman who's really working on her golf game might load up on lessons while one who's cheating might limit herself. You don't flaunt your extramarital affairs at clubs like Broken Oak, where too many old bluenoses live in disproportionate fear that some young dish is after their balding, impotent husbands. You are very discreet. Word gets around anyway, seems like.

Leafing through Jones's appointment book, I also noticed that Mrs. Fitch's name was gradually abbreviated, as Jones had done with Mrs. O, leading me to believe the big O stood for orgasm. The first few weeks it was Mrs. Fitch, then Mrs. F, and finally a big F. Meaning, for Broken Oak bluenoses, familiar? Or something even more familiar? I drove to her house in Centre Island.

Blue-collar Bayvilleites, like me, have trouble spelling Centre Island. It's that phony-baloney English thing. Centre Island's very existence is also enigmatic. It's a mere spit of sand jutting into Long Island Sound, just beyond Bayville, its homes protected from riffraff like me by a gatehouse and round-the-clock guards. Though I had a bona fide appointment to see Mrs. Fitch, the guard at the gatehouse, a retired cop, acted like he was doing me a favor to let me in.

Each house on Centre Island is bigger and better than the next. Dr. Fitch is a rich son of a bitch, who can easily afford to bust lots of golf clubs. Can I bust him for murder? His property had two driveways. One led to the front of the house, the other to the service entrance. I chose the former, though the charges made by service persons and homicide cops can both be murder.

Fitch's house was about the size of O'Reilly's, but you couldn't find a blade of crabgrass in the lawn and the gardens were edged with a laser. I parked near the front door, hopped out of my car, and suddenly became aware of another presence.

"Detective Kanopka?" A childlike voice wafted from behind a weeping cherry tree that could have made the cover of *Horticulture* magazine.

I turned to face a lovely young blond, probably a Swedish au pair, parting the cherry boughs like a beaded curtain.

"I'm here to see Mrs. Fitch," I said.

"That would be me," said the blond. At the sight of my surprise, she continued, "Don't worry, Detective. I'm often mistaken for my husband's daughter. I don't mind in the least."

Bet it bothers your ill-tempered hubby.

"Is he home?"

"He's operating."

"So you can't be his nurse," I said.

"I was," she admitted. "He left his first wife for me. The one who helped him earn his way through med school. I know it's a cliché. Now she's a castoff. Probably homeless and roaming the streets. While I've got all this."

"You knew Mr. O'Reilly?"

"The lush? The deadbeat? The pig?"

"So you did know him." She described his shortcomings so matter-of-factly, I responded in kind, though I must have sounded ridiculous.

"Thankfully," she said, "not so well."

"Did he ever make a pass at you?"

"He wouldn't have dared."

"Did you know Al Jones?" Let's see how matter-of-fact she can be about the tall Texan.

"I took golf lessons from him, but I strongly suspect you already knew that."

"Were you lovers?"

"Come on, Detective. You can do better than that. Boffing the golf pro's just another cliché. Am I a suspect?" She must have worked in the ER, the way she remained so calm under my questioning.

"Your husband is a suspect," I told her.

"Save yourself the trouble and the embarrassment, Detective. My husband is a great cardiologist. He saves lives. He doesn't take them."

"Maybe not," I said, producing a ballpoint and a small spiral pad, pretending to take notes, attempting to increase her emotion and her wariness. "But his temper's notorious," I added.

"Only on the golf course," she said, glancing at my pad. "Breaking a few clubs here and there is harmless and cathartic."

"Where was he last night?" I asked.

"Right here, with me." Mrs. Fitch defiantly placed her hands on her svelte hips. "We have help who can verify that."

I jotted "HELP!" on my pad, more as a cry than as a reminder to question her domestics.

"We found another body at Broken Oak," I told her, defiantly dotting the 'i' in her last name, which I had scribbled for no reason.

"Was he a member," she asked, as coolly as if admitting a John Doe to the hospital morgue, "or part of the staff?"

It seemed that she and her husband, both cool customers, were made for each other. But she had slipped up. "How do you know it's a man?" I asked, stopping my scribbling.

"I had to call it something," she told me, hands still on hips. "But what makes you think my husband had anything to do with it?"

I frowned, thinking, what makes you think the best defense is an offense? The more you rile me up, the more likely I'll run you in. Now I'll run you over to my car, where I'll show you the golf shoes with the missing heel spike.

"Recognize this?" I asked, handing one of the shoes to her.

"It's a golf shoe," she said, examining it more closely than I thought she would. "My husband's size, 10-D, like millions of other men."

"Most women don't know their husband's shoe size," I said, though I was not certain. "Do you buy his shoes and clothing?"

"Sometimes," she said. "Surgeons are often too busy saving lives to go shopping."

"I get the message," I told her. "And you're Florence Nightingale, but did you buy these?"

"How should I know? I've bought him several pairs of golf shoes in the past. I can't possibly recall when or where. He goes through them so fast. He throws them out long before he wears them out, or gives them away, believing that new equipment makes him play better. If you were a golfer, you would understand."

I can also understand his breaking clubs, though I can't afford the luxury. But I was still interested in her golf lessons.

"Did Al Jones help your game, or was it too tough to concentrate?" I asked, picturing him reaching around her from behind, adjusting her grip, starting her swing, touching just the right places.

She laughed, as if I had dubbed a shot and scattered the gallery.

"We have a witness who saw you and Jones together the night Mr. O'Reilly was murdered," I continued.

She laughed again and said, "There was a cocktail party. Lots of people could have seen us together, talking about my golf lessons."

"Our witness also saw you two out on the course," I said. "I suppose you were getting some air," I added, "or working on your sand shots."

"Don't be ridiculous, Detective. It was too dark."

"Not so dark that our witness couldn't see you and your golf pro getting it on in one of the sand traps."

"That's disgusting," she said, throwing the shoe at me. She turned and ran toward the house.

Only then did I notice her badly bruised, dark purple cheekbone, barely hidden under a thick layer of makeup.

CHAPTER FORTY-THREE

I had no witness who had seen Al Jones and Mrs. Fitch getting it on in the sand trap. That was all a bluff. You could call it entrapment. I needed to see her reaction. I don't think she whacked anyone, but her husband could have been looking for her and Jones out on the course in the dark, found O'Reilly peeing into the water hazard, and whacked him instead. Then Fitch could have come back and whacked Jones a few nights later, when Gregory, out collecting golf balls, spotted him. Then he went after the cousin, causing his heart attack, planting the five iron in his hands instead of his cranium. Is Dr. Fitch really Dr. Death? But why would Fitch make the neat trail of golf balls?

On my way home that evening, I stopped at the Tides and spied Mrs. O crossing Bayville Avenue. Headed toward the beach, she did not see me. I hopped out of my car and followed her.

Except for a lone fisherman casting into the water, the beach was deserted. The tide was high and the sun was setting. Long Island Sound rolled and glowed like a pool of liquid mercury. Maybe it is liquid mercury, considering the pollution.

Despite the Sound's metallic content and occasionally high coliform count, Bayville has a great beach for sunning and swimming. Unlike the ocean, there's no undertow and no breakers. Including the ball breakers that harried homicide cops endure constantly. I often strolled the beach on quiet evenings, after long, frustrating days on the job.

Mrs. O was about a hundred yards ahead of me, minding her own business, admiring the sunset. I scurried after her like a fiddler crab, my cop brogans filling with sand. Sensing someone behind her, she turned and looked surprised to see me.

"Am I under arrest?" she asked. "Or is this some sort of stakeout? Or maybe cops also like sunsets?"

"You ask a lot of questions."

"For a murder suspect, or someone you just made love with?" She slipped her hands into the back pockets of her khaki shorts, threatening to poke her braless breasts through her thin cotton T-shirt. It was a shirt advertising a Daytona Beach bikers' bar. She must be too young for me.

"I think I know the killer," I said.

"Oh?" She seemed unconcerned.

"It's Randy Randall's cousin."

"Who's that?"

"A mentally retarded, morbidly obese relative Randall kept locked up."

"Isn't that illegal?"

"His murder is. He was found this morning out on the golf course. He apparently suffered a heart attack."

Mrs. O whispered, "That's not murder" and continued admiring the sunset. Besides being too young, she could be too smart for me.

"He was clutching a five iron," I added. "Probably the murder weapon for the two others."

"What does that prove?" she said, cross-examining me as Carol used to. "And why would he have killed my husband?" Carol could always sense when I was on shaky ground.

"He felt threatened," I said, watching Mrs. O's reaction instead of the setting sun. "He believed that your husband would have razed Broken Oak and erected condos, though he only left his room late at night to raid the refrigerators and collect lost golf balls."

"How could he see them?"

"How could he miss them?"

"What do you mean?"

"Those refrigerators are huge." I smiled at my little joke, but Mrs. O frowned. Like Carol, she was better than me at staying on the investigative track.

"He may have had a flashlight," I added. "I'll check it out."

"If he only left his room late at night," she asked, "how did he know who my husband was?"

"Maybe he saw a photograph from the club roster," I tried. Though there were no club rosters in Gregory's room, or any photographs.

"Let me get this straight," she said. "He recognized my husband from a puny snapshot in a club roster, and knew it was him in the dark?"

"You a lawyer?" I said.

"Why would he have killed Al Jones?" said Mrs. O.

"There's no apparent motive," I admitted, picking up a smooth rock, trying to skim it. It disappeared after only one bounce. One bounce and you're out? A metaphor for my recently revived sex life?

"You know Mrs. Fitch?" I asked.

"We spoke a few times. Very briefly. Mostly going to and from our tables in the Broken Oak dining room. She never had much to say. Her husband did all the talking. She's much younger. I think he smothers her. I know nothing about him. Call it a woman's intuition, but I don't think he's a nice person."

That seemed to be a pretty good appraisal, though I'm wary of anyone telling me more than I ask for. "Ever notice anything unusual about her appearance?" I asked. "Any cuts or bruises?"

"You think he beat her?" Mrs. O raised an eyebrow, making me wonder if her husband had ever gotten rough with her.

"She's got a hell of a shiner," I said.

"I only noticed," sighed Mrs. O, "that she's a natural blond."

Now she's telling me too little, making me even warier, causing me to ask the salient question, "Did you know she was having an affair with Al Jones?"

"Am I supposed to be jealous?"

"You tell me."

"Despite what you may think," Mrs. O said, measuredly, staring at me instead of the sunset, "I was only interested in golf lessons."

"What about Dr. Fitch?"

"He's not my type."

Though that's not what I meant, at least I was pleased to hear it. "I was referring to Fitch's business dealings with your husband," I said.

"I thought Randall's cousin was the killer," said Mrs. O.

"You and everyone else," I said, trying to skim another rock. Watching it sink without a single bounce.

CHAPTER FORTY-FOUR

I left Mrs. O at the beach and went home with a headache. I looked for some aspirin in my medicine cabinet and found only an empty bottle. I found a few loose tablets in my golf bag in a pocket I stuff with tees, balls, gloves, socks. Can old socks enhance acetylsalicylic acid? Like hooch aged in old oaken casks? I also found, in another pocket, the last page of *Murder on the Moor*, mingling with an old jockstrap. Can old jocks enhance murder mysteries? Or solve them?

I swallowed two tablets and uncrumpled the last page. I had to read it, though my head throbbed and I had no idea how the page got in my golf bag. Peter H. Couloir had gathered all his suspects into one room, no mean feat, and explained that the evil earl of Cranbrook, whom I had suspected all along, did not murder Marty Phelps out on the moor, then murder Algernon Spotswood and stuff his body into a steamer trunk on the Orient Express. Couloir had also exonerated the earl's weird uncle Esmond, though he was holding the smoking gun, and accused Mrs. Phelps of engineering some sort of plot. He based his entire theory on a single whiff of Mrs. Phelps's perfume and the antifem-inist opinion that her dainty digits could not have handled the considerable recoil of a Webley-Vickers .44. Mystery buffs may be used to such machinations, but they boggle the mind of modern-day homicide cops. Anyway, I started reading.

". . . *your gamekeeper." Couloir looked at the Earl, then at Mrs. Phelps. "And your lover," he told her.*

"Preposterous!" said the Earl. "This young man has been in my employ for nearly seven years. He is scrupulously honest and his conduct is impeccable."

So was Ted Bundy's.

"Outrageous!" said Mrs. Phelps. "I loved my husband."

"Among others."

Atta boy, Couloir.

"It would not be indiscreet for me to observe," Couloir contin-ued, "that you had several affairs during the past few years. Un-fortunately for you, they were highly publicized."

"Au contraire, M. Couloir. The openness, shall we say, of my indiscretions, as you call them, only served to, shall I say, enhance my public appeal."

"As your voice was beginning to falter?"

"Be that as it may . . ." though obviously more concerned with her waning operatic career than with any indiscretions, Mrs. Phelps boldly continued, ". . . my husband was not averse to my taking a lover."

The voice is always first to go.

"Don't I have something to say in this?" said the gamekeeper.

Couloir ignored him, and said to Mrs. Phelps, "But you could not abide your husband's insistence on your retirement from the stage?"

"What about me?" the gamekeeper insisted.

Mrs. Phelps said to Couloir, "How did you know about that?"

Couloir said, "So you put this poor young man up to murdering your husband. Whereupon, M. Spotswood learned of your plot, threatened to blackmail you, and you did him in. Then you tried to make it look as if poor, deranged Esmond had murdered them both. Withal, one must remember that your husband's insistence on your retirement, not mere money, was your motive."

"How did you know?" pleaded Mrs. Phelps.

Couloir simply said, "I didn't."

Finis.

I think that means the end. I like the idea of combining a whiff of perfume with a big bluff to break a tough case. But to a modern cop, it seems like alchemy. I doubt it would work on someone as sharp as Mrs. Phelps. I'm trying my best to suspend disbelief, as my wife often urged me. After twenty years in homicide, however, I've learned not to believe anything or anybody. Or that such a bluff as Couloir's would ever work on Dr. Fitch, who's sharper than a scalpel.

CHAPTER FORTY-FIVE

"Want to see the corpse?" the ME said.

"No thanks," I said.

"Aw, come on. It's a major excavation. I had to cut through a foot of flab to get into his chest cavity. You wouldn't believe the size of his heart."

"Enlarged?"

"Ever heard that country song 'Heart Like a Whale'?"

"I only need to know if he died of a heart attack," I said.

"Long overdue," the ME said. "What a great place to drop dead. I can still see those fairways, rolling like tropical seas, those greens more even than pool tables. I assume he didn't play. What a shame. He was already in heaven."

"Was he running?" Tell me something I don't know.

"Maybe," the ME shrugged, "though it wouldn't have been very fast."

"What about the trail of golf balls?"

"What about them?"

"Okay. Here's an easier question. Were they his balls?"

"His prints are on some of them. Only his, as far as we can tell. The dimples don't make it easy. We're still checking. As for the balls belonging to him, I can show you the only ones I'm sure of. Enter the greatest autopsy room on earth," the ME said, like a sideshow barker. "Only one thin dime to see the fat man."

"What about the blood on the five iron he was holding?" I asked.

"Type O," he said. "Same as the second murder victim."

"Al Jones," I said, knowing he only cares about the numerical order of his corpses.

"The first victim was type A."

"O'Reilly," I said.

"That's backward," said the ME.

"How so?" I asked.

"It should have been A for Al and O for O'Reilly," he grinned.

I looked at the guy, young, attractive, but obviously spending too much time with corpses. I forced a smile. Though I didn't like the young prick much, I wouldn't want to have his job.

"We're doing the DNA matching," he explained. "As you know, it takes some time. But you've got your killer. Wanna see him? I had to put two autopsy tables together."

"I'm not so sure he's the killer."

A diploma, displayed on the wall behind the ME's desk, suddenly caught my attention. I squinted at it and said, "This looks like it's printed in Polish."

"If it were Polish," the ME said, "it would be hung upside down."

I looked closer. "Looks like this one's signed by, does that say Dr. Fitch?"

"He was formerly dean of my medical school. He's a great cardiologist."

So I've been told, by his doting wife. "Did he ever examine the fat cousin?"

"How should I know?"

"Would he know that any exertion could kill him?"

"Of course," said the ME. "Any cardiologist would have known."

CHAPTER FORTY-SIX

The five iron found on Randy's cousin had been purchased at Norm Harvey's Discount Golf Outlet in Jeri-
cho, confirmed by a computer trace of the serial number on
the shaft. Computers are great, but I still have to do the legwork, no matter how many bits and bytes back me up.

Norm's had no customers when I arrived. Two salesmen,
who were sipping coffee and shooting the breeze, pounced
on me.

"Can we help you?" the older one asked. He wore gobs of
gold jewelry, an obvious toupee, and a pencil moustache. I
might buy a set of irons from him, but never a used car. His
name was Herman.

"Where is everybody?" I asked. "It's still golf season."

"It's always golf season," said Herman's counterpart.

"Of course," Herman said. "We got one customer who
plays at least a hundred times a year. Lee Smith."

"What does he do for a living?" I asked.

"That's what his boss wants to know," Herman said. "Lee
was in yesterday, and he bought our last dozen copies of *Zen*

and the Art of Golf Cart Maintenance, by the Maharishi. He also bought the only Saddam Hussein autograph driver in existence, the Mother of All Clubs. I thought we'd never sell it, considering the obvious, plus it cost more than a Kuwaiti oil rig. But don't get me wrong," Herman continued. "Lee's a great guy. Very patriotic. Even his balls are red, white, and blue."

"Can you help me?" I flashed my ID.

"Why not? We get lots of cops in here."

"There are lots of these stores, aren't there?"

"Biggest chain in the country," Herman assured me. "If you're looking for Norm, he's not here, or at any of his other stores. On days like this, he's out playing golf."

"What about this?" I said, showing him the five iron.

"No returns," Herman shook his head. "All sales are final."

"I only want to know if it was bought here."

"Why didn't you tell me? Norm's always kept impeccable records, since the day he and his wife started this business out of their garage. Actually, Joyce kept the records. She's also steadier on the links. We should be called Joyce's Discount Golf."

Herman checked the five iron's serial number in their database, saying, "Computers don't lie. We know everything about our customers. Even the number of times they get laid. Here it is. Pretty quick, huh?" He printed out a sales slip and handed it to me.

I read that a full set of irons, including the five iron the fat cousin was holding, had been purchased there a week prior to O'Reilly's murder by Dr. Fitch.

"Great irons," Herman said. "You should buy a set. I'll throw in a free copy of Norm Harvey's book, *All I Know About Golf*."

"Let me guess," I said. "All the pages are blank?"

"Let's just say that Norm's game is a work in progress," said Herman. "By the way, what did this doctor who bought the irons do wrong?"

"You writing a book?" I said.

Herman nodded.

"Let's just say you should leave this chapter out," I told him, leaving him looking blank.

CHAPTER FORTY-SEVEN

Could Randy Randall's cousin have found the five iron when he was out collecting golf balls? Not likely. We scoured the place. And supposedly he did not collect clubs. At least there were none in his room. I decided to question Randy about this plus a couple of other inconsistencies. I found him in his office, sitting behind his antique desk, sipping fancy tea from a bone china cup that's too delicate to use in the main dining room.

"You sure there were never any golf clubs in Gregory's room?" I asked.

"Only balls," Randall said, savoring the words. Unlike the day before, his clothes were pressed, he was freshly shaved, and there were no bags under his eyes.

"Got a lost and found?"

He opened a closet behind his desk and withdrew a box containing a cashmere sweater, a pair of Ray-Bans, and a baseball cap with Donna Karan printed on the front.

"That's all?"

"Our members don't lose much."

But they've won life's lottery. Go figure.

"Nice sweater," I said, spreading it out.

"Embroidered with our Broken Oak logo," Randall said, as if I couldn't read. "Try it on, Detective. It's been here at least a month. If you don't want it, I'll toss it in the trash."

"I've got a sweater," I replied, more sharply than I meant to.

"Then one of our caddies will get it." Randall shrugged and sipped more of his tea, holding his pinkie at an angle I could never equal. "They're always going through the dumpster," he added.

"Al Jones have a lost and found in the pro shop?" I asked.

"I've already told you, Detective, our members don't lose much." Randall spoke like his jaw's wired shut and he should be sipping his tea through a straw.

"I disagree," I said sharply, meaning it this time.

"Oh?" He set his cup back in its saucer so they clattered.

"Dr. Fitch is notorious for losing his temper," I said. "It's also called self-control."

"In his defense, however," said Randall, "I must point out that he has a perfectly controlled bedside manner."

"How do you know?"

"Hearsay only. I know it's inadmissible in a court of law."

"I hear that he examined your cousin." Another bluff. Why not? Peter H. Couloir didn't invent it.

"So he did, a few weeks ago. During the August heat wave when Gregory was having chest pains."

"Correct me if I'm wrong, but most doctors don't make house calls."

"Dr. Fitch was here, having dinner in the club dining room. The diagnosis was heartburn. My cousin had eaten a whole roast beef, much to the chagrin of our chef, and no one knows how much Yorkshire pudding. The good doctor advised me to put him in the hospital for a thorough checkup, but Gregory wouldn't leave the premises." Gregory must have been a stubborn glutton.

"You could have ordered him to go."

"It's not that easy."

"It's also the height of the season." Goose Randy a little.

"Listen, Detective," Randall frowned. "I was never too busy for my cousin."

"Fitch must have known that any exertion could have killed Gregory."

"Who wouldn't?"

"Guess who owned the five iron your cousin was holding?"

"Dr. Fitch?"

"Good guess."

"He could have lost it."

"Isn't he a member?"

"Yes, but—"

"You said your members never lose anything."

"That's a priori reasoning, Detective."

"I flunked Latin. So I have to ask a lot of stupid questions."

"My supposition exactly." Randy was giving me his regular fish eye.

"Suppose you tell me how your cousin came by the club."

"He may have found it after Dr. Fitch flung it away in a fit of temper," Randall shrugged and gave me a look of dismissal.

"I considered that," I told him. "But you and I both know that your cousin did not collect golf clubs."

CHAPTER FORTY-EIGHT

How to catch Fitch? First, you row to his native habitat, in this case, Centre Island. Then you cast a line. Such as, Why did you hit your wife? And you wriggle the bait in front of his arrogant nose. But which bait—the shoes with the missing spike or the five iron? He can only strike at one at a time. Careful, Kanopka. Catch him by surprise.

Fitch's front door flew open before I could ring the bell.

"What is it this time?" he hissed at me, his eyes colder than a great white shark's.

"You knew I was here?" Was he holding a five iron behind the door?

"I have an electric eye for trespassers," he continued hissing. Unlike barking dogs, can hissing animals bite?

"Recognize these?" I showed him the golf shoes.

"Why should I?"

"Your wife told me they look like a pair she bought for you."

"That is not exactly a positive identification." He smiled slightly, or was it a wince, like the hook had been set?

"Positive enough, when linked with other evidence." I held the shoes against the door, so he couldn't slam it in my face.

"Evidence?"

"These shoes match a print by O'Reilly's body at the water hazard."

"So what?"

"The killer was wearing them."

"Where did you find them?"

"In Al Jones's locker."

"Then he is your killer."

"They don't fit."

"They were planted there?"

"Are they yours?"

Fitch gave me a look that said "Idiot," took a shoe from me, examined it, and said, "They look like a pair I once owned. They caused blisters. I threw them out." Was that before or after you smacked your wife? "At Broken Oak, I believe."

"Why?"

"I told you, they caused blisters."

Fitch handed back the shoe and said, "I am a busy man, Detective, as you must be, also. You must have more important things to do than keep me standing in my doorway."

"Not so fast," I said. "We also found your five iron."

"I have owned a lot of five irons over the years," he said, evenly.

"It's the one that killed Jones and O'Reilly," I told him.

"Are you certain it belonged to me?" he said. Trying to trip me up, like a shaky med student during an oral exam. Although *his* blood pressure seemed to be rising.

"We know exactly when and where you bought it," I said. "Right to the second and the salesclerk. You bought it the week before Mr. O'Reilly was murdered."

"I also lost it that week. If you must know, Detective, I threw that five iron into the woods."

"Near the water hazard where O'Reilly's body was found?"

"I cannot recall." Fitch's jaw clenched, like he was biting the hook.

"You seem to have an otherwise excellent memory," I said, keeping the line taut. "Did anyone see you throw it?"

"I was playing solo," said Fitch, twisting the doorknob so it seemed it might come off. "With a caddy, of course."

Walking the course, like the pros, so you get a better feel for it? That's the only way to play, though I'm my only caddy.

"Who was it?"

"Slim," Fitch seethed. "No one knows his real name. He wanted to retrieve the five iron, but I would not let him. When I let one fly, I never want to see it again."

"That's quite a temper," I said, reasonably sure that he did not have another five iron behind the door. The way his face was turning the color of the hot pink golf socks he was fond of wearing, he would have flung it by now.

"Are you implying that I could get mad enough to murder someone?"

"Someone like O'Reilly," I kept up the pressure, "who bilked you out of twenty grand."

"I save lives, Detective. I do not take them." Fitch's hands trembled on the doorknob.

"Or someone like Al Jones," I added, my foot between the door and the jamb.

"Why would I touch our late, revered golf pro?"

"For boffing your wife?"

"Boffing?" Fitch's forehead broke out in blotches.

"That's what I said." I withdrew my foot but not my words.

"You had better hope, for your sake, Detective, that expression only means giving her golf lessons."

He slammed the door in my face, after which I heard another door slam inside the house, and some breaking glass.

CHAPTER FORTY-NINE

"Stay away from Dr. Fitch," said a vaguely familiar voice, when I answered my phone later.

"Who is this?" I asked.

"Your kumpel."

"I should have known it was you, Kowalski, and I'm not your pal."

"But I'm your captain."

"And I'm in the privacy of my home this evening, off duty."

"Have another one, on me." He chortled. "And stay away from Fitch."

"You still believe that Randall's cousin is the killer?"

"Prints all over that five iron, along with the golf pro's blood, and ashes proving it's the same club that killed the mick, are pretty convincing. He was gonna raze Broken Oak, you dork."

"What happened to kumpel?"

"The fat cousin did it. Case closed."

"So he could keep raiding the Broken Oak kitchen instead of dumpster dining over in Glen Cove?"

"You'll always be a wiseass, Kanopka. And always a lieutenant."

"You're forgetting there's no way the fat cousin could have whacked a guy Jones's size, hauled his body to the Crown Vic, and dumped it into the trunk without having a massive heart attack."

Kowalski was silent a moment.

"Anyone there? I paid my phone bill this month."

"Stay away from Dr. Fitch," Kowalski repeated. "That's an order."

"I had to question him. It was his five iron."

"Let it go, Kanopka," Kowalski insisted. "Both our butts are on the line here. We got all the evidence we need on Randall's cousin, and Fitch is innocent. Stay away from him. That's final. Got me?"

"Someone's got you in their pocket," I said.

"I'll try real hard to forget you said that," said Kowalski and hung up.

CHAPTER FIFTY

I considered drinking myself catatonic, but instead drove to Broken Oak. Despite Kowalski's orders to leave well enough alone, I felt compelled to prowl the links at night. The tenth hole water hazard, where O'Reilly bought the farm. The recently seeded areas, where Al Jones most likely bit the dust. The sixth fairway, where Randall's fat cousin infarcted. If I could find them in the dark, I could put myself in the victim's shoes, get the feel of the killer stalking me. Take a deep, cleansing breath before arresting him. In case Kowalski's right and I'm dead wrong.

It was half-past nine but the parking lot was filled with cars. The dining room had reopened and every table looked filled. They were having a buffet, free margaritas, and a lot of noise and merriment. I ventured down a cart path, past the practice putting green and pro shop, toward the mansion's rear patio, where some of the beau monde were dining alfresco amid twinkling lights and clinking silverware. From my vantage point below, on the cart path in darkness, the members resembled passengers on the *Titanic*. Dr. and

Mrs. Fitch were seated by the railing, at a table set with starched white linen and fresh-cut flowers, along with two other couples. All were laughing at some anecdote related by the evil doctor. About getting away with murder?

I see you, and I see right through you, I thought. Your arrogance and smugness. Believing you're God Almighty. Keep laughing, Doctor, but you're as mortal as this lowly detective. You and your ilk can't save supermarket green stamps when God intervenes. Your ilk couldn't save my wife, damn you. Now I'm hot on your trail like the hound of hell. Keep laughing, though you just glimpsed me, crouched like a gargoyle on a gutter spout, about to bring you down.

CHAPTER FIFTY-ONE

I wandered onto the golf course in the moonless night. There was also no moon for all three murders. Fitch must have good night vision. I stayed to the middle of the fairways, like good golf shots, wary of stumbling into sand traps, tripping over sprinkler heads, yardage markers. The killer has to know the course by heart. To me, it was like entering the heart of darkness. A bad read for cops, forced on me by my wife. Art should be uplifting, like Chopin, though his nocturnes can put me to sleep as quickly as Conrad. Let's face it. They were both pretentious Polacks. My wife was a nocturne, but I'll always be a polka.

I imagined myself as the killer, trying to get into his mind. Stalking my victims. Despising them. Becoming one with the darkness. Letting all the evil in the world flow through me. Gleefully whacking O'Reilly by the water hazard. Coldly cutting down Al Jones. Callously chasing Randall's cousin to a horrid, gasping death.

I stared at the faraway sea of stars, fearing that one would suddenly flare down, disclosing me like a searchlight. I recalled Carol once telling me, after reading the *Science Times* section, that the stars are racing away from us. Something called the red shift, expanding the universe into complete darkness.

Evil adores darkness and loathes men like Peter H. Couloir, men capable of cutting through chaos and obfuscation, through clouds of gunpowder filled with leaden comets. Men with computer-like minds, little gray cells, detecting delicate scents such as Eau de la Nuit, and performing alchemy to find a killer. Men with minds like satellite dishes, ever open to case-breaking insights and single flickers from the farthest stars. But what about men like me, Detective Wiseass, with only brass balls and alcohol haze to help me?

Out there on the Robert Trent Jones–designed course— where every hole should be a hard par but an easy bogey, unless you leave in a body bag—instead of feeling like the killer, I suddenly felt like someone who'd kicked himself loose from the earth. If the hot-tempered Dr. Fitch, after glimpsing me on the cart path in the dark, had left the twinkling patio lights and his terribly bright dinner companions and called Kowalski, again complaining of continuing harassment, I might as well kick myself loose from twenty-plus years in homicide and my pension.

I found the tenth hole water hazard by stepping in it. It was blacker than black. Had O'Reilly also stepped into it? Was the weight of the world also on his shoulders when he did? Could he hear his heart beating like a tribal drum? Did he know he was being stalked, like a lone kudu at the last watering hole on the Serengeti? Had the scents and sounds of his pissing attracted his attacker? Did he know deep down, in the pit of his dark developer's heart, that there was no hope? Or was he just another happy drunk? Whether or not he'd stepped into this water hole by accident, he stepped into deep shit. As I was about to.

Wetting my feet made me want to piss. What the hell. I may as well flash the frogs with my impotence in solving these murders. At least pissing feels useful and good. How many members have thusly watered this course?

Aaah, that *is* good. No doubt the greenskeeper and his crew, most of the caddies, maybe even Al Jones, have taken leaks out here from time to time. I bet that more than a few women have relieved themselves behind a convenient tree or bush. If they used a sand trap, did they rake it afterward, as the little signs remind? The vision made me smile a little.

Could the sound of my stream carry all the way back to the patio? Though it's almost as loud and strong as waiters pouring big pitchers of ice water, I doubt it. At least I don't have a prostate problem. Though Dr. Fitch may suspect otherwise and offer me a free exam, using a hand grenade instead of his middle finger.

I shook the last few drops, zipped back up, and continued wandering in the darkness. Beyond the primal sounds of my urine, the course was dead silent and growing even darker. The kind of dark that makes you wonder if you're awake or still having a nightmare. I encountered a mass, not far from the water hazard, looming like a burial mound. A high tee, I recalled, for launching little white balls up and out over the water hazard. Judging by the number of balls we found in the drink while fishing for five irons, however, high tees don't help most of the club golfers.

I followed a steep, winding path behind the mound to the elevated tee. I had followed it before in daylight and was almost sure of my footing. When I got to the top, I should have been able to see the roof of the clubhouse above the treetops.

The last ten yards of the path was a stairway made from railroad ties, heading straight up. I tripped on the first step but quickly recovered my balance and bounded up the rest, all the way to the top, without losing any breath. And they say that golfers are not real athletes.

From the elevated tee, the course looked like the dark side of the moon. Even so, I could differentiate between certain shadows and make out the water hazard. It looked like a black hole or a pool of India ink. I'll leave the similes to the likes of Dame Winifred. *Vraiment le coeur de la nuit,* Peter H. Couloir might say.

Someone standing atop the tee, even on the darkest night, could still see, and certainly hear, someone pissing into the water hazard. They could also see the sand trap where Al Jones and Mrs. Fitch were getting it on.

Stepping toward the edge of the tee for a closer look, I tripped over a tee marker and fell flat. I laughed at myself, until I felt my ankle. It hurt like hell. I had twisted it once before, on a golf course of all places, and was on crutches for weeks. And they say that golf's not rough.

I rubbed the ankle, worried about being stranded all night in this blackness until Vince Henry, swinging his antique scythe and grinning like Freddie Kruger, found me at the crack of dawn. Or until Dr. Fitch found me, hopefully with his dawn patrol foursome, so he couldn't finish me off.

I was not alone, however. A shadow suddenly moved and I sensed another presence, crouched beyond the edge of the slope down to the water hazard. "Who's there?" I called out.

No answer.

Whoever it was had come up the slope, which was steep and difficult to climb. Don't they know about the stairway of railroad ties? The figure moved again.

"Who's there?" I repeated.

Again, no answer.

It was too big to be an animal, unless it was a bear. But there are very few wild animals on Long Island, unless you count drivers on the LIE and shoppers at the Roosevelt Field Mall.

"Don't worry," I said, thinking it must be a kid who'd been sitting up there smoking pot. "I won't bust you for trespassing or anything. I need some help. I've fallen and I can't get up."

Jeez. I can't believe I said that.

The shadow lengthened, steadily upward, swaying like a bear that's trying to stand on its hind legs. Kid's still scared, I thought, until the shadow lunged at me.

"Here's all the help you'll need," Slim, the caddy, whispered, swinging a golf club at my head.

"Shit!" I shouted, trying to get up, tripping again, so he landed only a glancing blow.

"Dig in, motherfucker," he spat. "Here comes eternity." He loomed over me like a rabid grizzly and raised the club.

I managed to pull my snub-nose from its holster, but Slim's next swing caught me on the wrist and launched the pistol into the darkness.

"Hole in one," he said, waving the club like he'd just won the Ryder Cup.

"Aaagh!" I shouted. My wrist now hurt more than my head and ankle. The pain was getting progressively worse. One more swing could send me into shock. Do something, Kanopka. But what? My right eye filled with blood, distorting my depth perception even more than the darkness, and I was still on the ground. As Slim swung the club at me again, it was all I could do to cross my arms.

"Take that, you friggin' pig!"

The blade of the club bit into my forearm, audibly cracking a bone. I thought irrationally it must be a Cobra and

242

tried grabbing it, but Slim was able to take another back swing.

"You can't escape," he hissed, seemingly crazed by the scent of my blood as he angled for another, deadlier divot.

I rolled as he swung and missed. Then I hopped to my feet, though the pain in my ankle was excruciating. No way I could run. I thought of lunging at him, like a desperate prizefighter, and getting inside his long arms. I could even try biting off his ear. But Slim swung again, too soon. I hopped backward, tripped over a bench, and fell flat on my back. His deadly blade whispered past my ear, biting only air this time.

"You're lucky," Slim said, panting from the effort. I could almost smell the cheap wine and cigarettes on his breath. "But now your luck's run out."

"What do you consider unlucky?" I said. Aching all over, shaking with fear, biding for time.

"You ain't dead yet," he grinned. At least I think he grinned, but the darkness hid his rotten teeth.

"You can't kill a cop," I pleaded. "You get the death penalty."

Slim gave a last crazy laugh and shouldered the Cobra like Barry Bonds with a Louisville Slugger. I feebly crossed my arms again, expecting more pain, until a clanging sound came. The clang of metal hitting metal, not flesh and bone.

"What the—"

Slim's swing had connected with a ball washer near the end of the bench, instead of my cranium, snapping the blade off his club. As he stared disbelievingly, I gathered my wits, along with my brass balls, and told him, "You're under arrest."

"You're gonna get pinned like a friggin' butterfly," he said, aiming the broken end of the shaft at me.

I twisted and rolled as Slim stabbed the turf. He was better at swinging complete clubs. I made it to my knees, managed to spring straight up at the tall caddy, and wrapped a bear hug around his chest. He dropped the shaft and pummeled me with half punches. I hung on to him for dear life. His arms and shoulders were strong from carrying all those golf bags. If he landed a roundhouse and knocked me out, he'd surely grab the shaft and stab me through the heart.

"Let go!" he shouted.

I obliged by throwing my best left hook at his temple. It should have decked him, but he was still standing. So I punched his dark heart, and we tumbled off the tee together. And they say that golf is not a contact sport.

CHAPTER FIFTY-TWO

I broke my ankle. Slim broke my forearm and put fifty stitches in my scalp. I managed to restrain him until the cops came, thanks to my dexterity with handcuffs in the dark, which had not come from anything kinky. And thanks to Dr. Fitch, who had called Kowalski to complain that I was harassing him. I wonder if my kumpel would have sent a patrol car so fast if he knew I was getting my head handed to me. He and Gleason will never change. Both captains will always bow to political pressure, and I'll always be a lieutenant. They were also relieved that Fitch was not the killer, while I regretted it, and they were pleased that Slim confessed to everything, though it proved them wrong about Randy Randall's cousin Gregory.

Grinning like we were giving him a green jacket for winning the Masters instead of a straitjacket, Slim told our interrogating team about his "night game." About playing the Broken Oak links after dark and beating all the legends, from Bobby Jones to Tiger Woods, unaware that it was only shadow golf. I often imagine myself as a great golfer, a legend in my own mind, but the next shot usually brings me back to reality.

Slim also told us that O'Reilly had promised to back him on the pro tour. What a cruel joke. I was almost convinced that O'Reilly deserved getting whacked and Slim should get a reduced sentence, until he confessed to killing Al Jones, believing he should be the pro at Broken Oak instead of Jones. After caddying for Jones in the Long Island Open, Slim was convinced he could beat him. Puh-leese. It takes a lot more than shadow golf. Slim had the added incentive of a failed blackmail attempt, after spying Jones and Mrs. Fitch getting it on in the bunker. As Slim revealed, "Damn tight Texan wouldn't fork over so much as a friggin' fin for me to keep my mouth shut." He would not admit, however, to chasing cousin Gregory to death. "The fat dude was already dead when I found him," Slim insisted. "I only planted the five iron on him, and left the trail of golf balls outa respect. He couldn't play a lick, but he had his own night game goin' with collectin' them friggin' balls."

Gregory was buried in the family plot at Locust Valley Cemetery, beside his aunt Dame Winifred. I wanted to attend the funeral, to pay my respects and see if Gregory was meeting his maker in a piano crate, but I was in too much pain. Two weeks later, however, I made it to the memorial service Randy Randall held on the first tee at Broken Oak. I must admit that I was mostly paying my respects to the great game of golf, while hoping that Randall would invite me to play that fabulous course, when I could walk.

I crutched from my car to the first tee, wondering how my wounds would affect my swing. Ben Hogan was never the same after the car accident that nearly killed him. Randall and a local minister were there, trading homilies through their Locust Valley lockjaw, oblivious to the heavenly fairway behind them. Gleason and Kowalski stood off to the side, patting themselves on the back. There were several others I had never seen, most likely Randall's out-of-town relatives, plus a few curious members. They were also memorializing O'Reilly and Al Jones, but I did not expect an overflow crowd. Few knew Gregory, fewer liked O'Reilly, and though Jones may have had a sizable fan club, consisting mostly of lonely women, his body had been shipped back to the Longhorn State.

I failed to notice Vince Henry until I reached the tee. The greenskeeper's tailored business suit, minus his black baseball cap with the big white X, made him look almost like a member. Fat chance. Vince will get into Broken Oak when women are admitted to Augusta National.

"Been there, done that," the burly ex–football player said to my crutches, "when I blew out my knees."

"Paying your respects," I said, "or looking for job security?"

Vince bristled, then chuckled. "Gotta do what you gotta do," he said. "Bet no one knows that better than you."

The comment caused me to glance at Gleason and Kowalski, who waved for me to join them. Considering my crutches, they should have come to me. They may want to tell me something that Vince shouldn't hear, I considered. But they had already told the whole world how brilliant they were to keep me on the case when I was floundering, and how they had always suspected that Slim was the killer. "It was risky sending Karl out on the course at night by himself," they repeatedly told reporters, "but we needed a decoy." Though I made that dumb decision all by myself, I had decided not to dispute them. Why make waves? Why not be grateful they didn't let you nail Dr. Fitch, which would have killed your career, and let it go at that? You did come up smelling like a rose, though they're taking most of the credit. I hobbled toward them, doing what I gotta do, as Vince so aptly put it, and ran into Mrs. O.

"You look much better," she said, cutting me off from the captains, who collared someone else and started explaining how they broke the case.

"You told me you weren't coming," I told Mrs. O, whose sheer summer dress was more suited for a garden party than a memorial service.

"At the hospital," she shrugged, "you had more visitors than the pope. How could we talk about anything?"

I nodded and frowned. Even Dr. Fitch had dropped by while making his rounds. He enjoyed seeing me flat on my back and seemed more pleased with the course reopening than with the killer being caught. Where was he now? Out on the back nine? Back at the hospital? Beating his wife? She'd better not show up to mourn her golf stud.

"I suppose this is also no time to talk," Mrs. O added, "but you didn't call me."

"I just got out," I said. "I would have stopped later at the Tides."

"You would have missed me," she said. "I've already checked out."

"Where are you going?" I asked.

She was about to answer when Randy Randall and the minister accosted us.

"Sorry for your loss," one of them said. I'm not sure which one it was, as each spoke like a ventriloquist.

"Thank you," said Mrs. O, as demurely as her dress would allow.

"My only loss is my golf game," I said.

"When you are fully recovered," said Randall, "you must play here."

"Really?" I hadn't been angling for an invitation. Not yet.

"Any Monday," Randall added.

"Aren't you closed on Mondays?" the minister said.

"Our course will remain open for this detective," Randall said, "after all he has done for us."

We'll see about that. To Randall and the country club set, it will always be us and them.

"Then why not invite him when he can use the club-house?" said the minister. "He'll need to shower, change his clothes, get a bite to eat."

"Of course," Randall said, without missing a beat. "Why hadn't I thought of that?"

Thank God for the clergy, I thought, until Randall added, "We'll put him in a foursome with Dr. Fitch. They know each other."

I tried to smile. I'd rather play with Slim. There's no way Fitch wants to play with me either. When I recover, I'll opt for Mondays. I'll bring Enrique, maybe a couple of other cops, but I won't abuse the privilege.

"He'll fit right in with any foursome," the minister said. "Monday is when the caddies play."

"Not anymore," Randall said.

"Why not?" the minister asked.

"Let us just say," Randall lisped, "that Slim put a different slant on the situation."

"Poor, tortured soul," the minister intoned, putting his hands together as if praying. I would have commented negatively, to put it mildly, had he not done his best to try and upgrade my golf invitation.

"I suppose he's toast," Mrs. O said evenly.

"In this state?" I laughed.

"We do not enforce the death penalty," Randall said, like it's a good thing.

"An eye for an eye diminishes all of us," said the minister.

"Don't worry, he'll get life," I assured them. "The jury will be in tears when they learn how he lived in a dilapidated caddy shack, with only a small campfire to keep warm."

"What a shame." Randall clucked his tongue as if he had nothing to do with Slim's living conditions. He turned abruptly and headed toward a group of his relatives, taking the minister with him.

"Slim stoked his campfire with a five iron Dr. Fitch threw away in a fit of temper," I informed Mrs. O. "Ashes from the blade were in the head wounds of both murder victims."

"You must be a good detective," she said.

"Good detectives use their little gray cells to uncover the evidence," I admitted. "I need to get hit in the head with it. I was standing in those ashes when I first questioned Slim."

She laughed, tenderly touched my forearm cast, and asked, "May I sign?"

I thought she was kidding until she tugged at my jacket lapel, like she was starting to undress me. She plucked a ballpoint from my inside pocket, as comfortably as Carol would have done. As if we had been married for years, or at least had more than a one-night stand. I thought of commenting on our relationship, or lack thereof, but returned to the safer subject of murder.

"A lefty killed Al Jones and your husband," I said. "Slim's a lefty, but he plays righty golf."

"Okay to sign right here?"

"According to Slim, he could only manage to steal right-handed clubs as a kid. So that's how he plays. But when he swings them like a baseball bat, it's always lefty. I can vouch for that."

"Has he always been a caddy?" She started signing.

"And a drifter."

"You don't feel a little sorry for him?"

"It was a long time before I made enough money for good clubs," I said, "but I never stole any or murdered anyone. Lawyers are always coming up with that kind of crap," I added. "Switching sympathy from victims to criminals. Though I must admit that Slim did not have much of a life."

"Compared to a great detective?"

"Don't write anything like that. Remember the ashes?"

"Don't sell yourself short," said Mrs. O, as she finished signing. "There. How's that?"

"I can't read upside down," I said. Peter H. Couloir probably could, but he was a great detective.

"What about my drawing?" Mrs. O asked.

"It looks like a little palm tree," I said, twisting my forearm for a better look, though it hurt. "What does that mean?"

"I'm going back to Florida," she said, "the land of fresh starts, like the signs say down there."

"You can start fresh in Bayville," I said, wondering how far I would go to get her to stay. "I read somewhere that the chamber of commerce is putting up a sign."

Mrs. O laughed and said, "Florida's also got fresh orange juice."

"So does Bayville," I said, "but you have to squeeze it yourself." Carol used to squeeze mine. Could I let Mrs. O do it for me?

"I'm sick of living in a motel," she said.

"I've got a house," I shrugged, as if the front door had always been open, and Carol would understand my blatant invitation. "You could stay there."

"That's sweet," said Mrs. O, "but I couldn't impose."

"It's no imposition," I insisted, "and no commitment."

"Commitment's what I need. Oh, I didn't mean—"

"I know what you mean . . ." I hesitated a moment, pretending to read the message on my cast, and told her, "I think you mean, do we have anything in common beside murder and one night together in bed?"

"You are a good detective."

"You like Chopin?" I said. "You know, the Polack composer who wrote all those nocturnes?"

"I also like polkas," said Mrs. O, lightly touching my cast again. Letting me know I still had a chance.

"What about mystery novels?" I asked. "Where the murders occur around Gothic mansions like this one, and get solved in wood-paneled drawing rooms by impossibly clever, tweedy little tecs?"

"I do like mysteries," she admitted.

"What about golf?" I asked. "I'm a better teacher than any golf pro."

Mrs. O rolled her eyes, like I should be committed instead of Slim.

When the memorial service was over, Mrs. O and I went together to our cars. "Follow me," I said, stowing my crutches and levering myself into my driver's seat, careful of the cast on my right arm. The injury *could* help my golf game. My right arm's too strong and I tend to hook the ball.